MW00880254

Visions of Home

To my mother, Heather Meyers.
Thank you for sharing your love of romance with me.

"Heart of my own heart,
whatever befall,
still be my Vision,
O Ruler of all"
-Eleanor Hull, "Be Thou My Vision"

Chapter 1

It did not rain on the day her parents were buried. Their graves rested on a shallow hill in a little village located only a day-long carriage ride from Paris. Within the vibrant blue sky, the sun had shone through wispy summer clouds. In a green and flowery hillside below, crops continued to grow while creatures and villagers twittered about.

The funeral was small with just a priest, the head nun, and Clair in attendance. After the priest had ended his homily with the sign of the cross, he left the Mother Superior to watch over Clair as she grieved. Clair had bent to place a hand on the foot of the freshly dug mound.

"*Maman, Papa*, what shall I do now?" she'd asked. The Mother Superior rested a frail hand on the girl's shoulder.

"We were supposed to find our new home together," Clair explained while she wiped away a stray tear, "but we never had a chance to take a step out of our home village. How will I travel to America without them?"

She bowed her head, and a few tears trickled down her cheeks.

Over the following days, Clair continued to visit her parents' gravesite after completing her morning chores at the French convent. The nuns insisted she take a few days to rest and mourn, but Clair did not like to sit still. Keeping her hands busy was a good distraction. When all activity halted during the late morning prayers, woeful revelations permeated her mind, repeatedly reminding her that she was now alone in the world. While the nuns sang and read their *félicitations*, Clair trekked down the hillside adjacent to the cathedral. Headstones littered its grounds. The sun peaked its way through low-hanging clouds, encouraging the morning dew to rise to greet it. While weaving through the maze of chiseled stone and wood, Clair contemplated her bleak prospects. Being only fifteen years old with no relatives to care for her meant she could either stay at the convent or take her chances finding employment. She knew that becoming a maid or servant as an unmarried woman with no protection meant risking her safety. Many young girls would travel through her village seeking refuge because they had become pregnant by their masters. Her background would also increase the risk to her safety. Her mother had warned Clair of how people would treat her if they discovered the truth about her parents' history–a history they worked hard to keep secret.

Her mother had once said, "I had left that kind of situation, hoping my daughter would never experience such horrors."

Clair considered staying at the convent. She knew the nuns would gladly keep her. They were kind and did not care that she was unusual, but they required her to remain on the grounds, and she could not explore the woods or visit the nearby village. Her chances of leaving France and traveling to America would dwindle. She would not be able to raise funds, and the only way they would allow her to leave is if she found someone to support her. The only person she could imagine in that role was a husband, but, with her situation, finding a husband with the means to travel would be difficult, and she feared any other prospect would tie her down to France.

Clair's thoughts grew more melancholy the moment she spotted her parents' grave. The mound was still rounded and dark from the freshly-dug soil. She felt a weight on her chest as if she herself were buried under all that dirt. She feared her future would be dark and isolated. Overcome by grief, she lowered herself to the ground, heedless of sullying her skirt in the process. She was oblivious to her surroundings and, as such, did not hear footsteps behind her.

"Oh! This is truly unfortunate. I am too late," a feminine

voice said in Clair's native tongue of French, startling her out of her lament.

Clair adjusted herself and swiveled to see the source of the voice. Standing behind her was a petite, older woman with dark brown eyes and blonde hair. Her nose curved and her chin jutted out, giving her a constant sharp expression of pride. Her almond-shaped eyes and thick eyebrows reminded Clair of her father.

The woman frowned at the grave while the inner corners of her eyebrows were raised. Her one hand grasped a black parasol while the other fingered a necklace. Although she was dressed in simple traveling attire–a plain, thick, brown wool–the woman's parasol was made of fine material, and her gloves looked to be silk.

The Mother Superior, who had accompanied the woman, stepped between Clair and the stranger. She gave a reassuring smile.

"Hello, my child. I assumed you would be down here. I want to introduce you to Mrs. Nicollete Tailleur. She has traveled all the way from Paris. Mrs. Tailleur, this is Clair Delacourt."

At first, the strange woman kept her gaze on the grave before finally shifting her eyes to Clair. Her frown deepened as she appraised the girl before her.

"You are Philip's daughter?"

Clair nodded but remained mute. Her throat felt raw from crying, and she didn't trust her voice to emerge clearly in front of someone she didn't know.

"Your father sent me a letter almost a week ago," the woman continued. "He had informed me of his illness. I had hoped to arrive before his passing, but alas, I am too late." She sighed and paused a moment before continuing. "Now that he is dead, I am obligated to take you in as my ward. My husband is a man of great fortune, and we can provide for you until you find a suitable husband." Her eyes widened when she saw below Clair's knees. "My goodness, your dress is ruined." She stepped forward and grabbed Clair's arm to hoist her to her feet. Clair, shocked by the unexpected encounter, allowed her to assist with her standing, though she stumbled into an upright position. "This disregard for your appearance is unacceptable."

Once Clair had a firm footing, she wrenched her arm from the stranger's grasp.

"How do you know my father?" she demanded.

The woman's posture became rigid, and her hand curled into a fist. "How impertinent of you. I am your father's sister."

"My father had no sister. In fact, he had no living relatives." Clair looked to the Mother Superior, who calmly stood by, hoping for assistance.

"Clair," the Mother Superior explained, "Mrs. Tailleur has shown me the proper documents. She is, in fact, your father's sister."

"But that can't be!" Clair exclaimed. "My father would not lie to me!"

"You insolent child," exclaimed Mrs. Tailleur. "You should not talk back to your elders. This rude behavior must have come from your mother. My brother was considered a respectable gentleman–that is, until he married that heathen woman. I will be sure to teach you proper manners once we arrive in Paris."

"Ladies," the Mother Superior intervened, "why don't we take a moment to compose ourselves by returning to my office for some tea?"

Clair, ignoring the nun, struggled to contain her outrage. Her voice cracked as she spoke.

"How dare you call my mother a heathen! She was a kind and–"

"Comport yourself, girl! I am your aunt, and you will treat me with respect." She turned to the nun. "I apologize, Mother Superior. I had no idea how unruly her upbringing was. I appreciate your offer of tea, but I must respectfully decline. I think it's best we begin our travels as soon as possible. I would hate for her to cause a scene in the middle of the entire convent."

Clair took a step in the nun's direction. "Mother Superior, please don't make me go with this stranger. If you allow me to stay here, I will work hard to earn my keep."

The Mother Superior's wrinkled face showed sympathy. She placed a hand on Clair's shoulder. "My child, she is your aunt. She has the documents to prove it. By law, she has the right to take you into her home and care for you. This is very fortunate. With your age, it is better for you to accept the aid of your aunt and uncle. If you will not consider your own well-being, please consider your father's last wishes."

Clair took a step back. "What do you mean by my father's last wish?"

"Like your aunt explained, he sent her a letter before he passed." The Mother Superior turned to Mrs. Tailleur. "Do you have the letter with you? I think it would be beneficial if Clair read it."

The woman pulled a folded paper from beneath her belt, grumbling under her breath as she did so. As she extended the parchment toward Clair, she complained, "I don't know why I have to explain anything to her. She is only a child."

Clair ignored her protest and read the note.

My Darling Sister,

I know there has been much strife between us since my marriage. I wish we could have mended our estrangement while I was still alive. Unfortunately, my wife and I are gravely ill. We have a fifteen-year-old daughter who will soon be orphaned. I know you do not agree with my past choices, but please do not let her pay for my supposed sins. I implore you to take her in as your ward. She is currently residing at our village convent to prevent her from catching the disease. Please care for her as if she were your own. You and I were close as children, and I have faith you will love her as much as you once loved me.

Sincerely,
Your loving brother,

Philip Delacourt

Clair could not identify the handwriting on the note, but she recognized her father's signature. It was shaky and not straight, indicative of an unsteady hand ravaged by illness. A fresh set of tears welled in Clair's eyes. She bowed her head, letting her arms dangle at her sides. The letter fluttered to the foot of her parents' grave. Dread filled her stomach as the realization of her new reality became clearer. Her father's last wish was for her to go with this woman he called his sister. She did not want to go against his plans, and she trusted his judgment and knew he would only put in place what was best for her.

In the letter, he did not mention her aunt helping her travel to their planned destination in America. With that other realization, she knew that gone were her hopes and dreams. Gone were the plans her family had shared to find belonging in a newly changing country. Now she must live a lie among suffocating aristocrats with an aunt she did not know.

"It is as you say," Clair said. "I will do as my father wished."

"I am glad you came to your senses," her aunt replied as she brushed at her skirts. "Mother Superior, if you don't mind, I will take you up on that offer of tea after all. Afterward, we will pack the girl's belongings. My husband will not be pleased with me being away for so long, so we must start our travels as soon as possible."

"I understand," replied the Mother Superior. "Clair, I suggest you say your final goodbyes now."

Clair turned toward the grave and noticed the letter laying atop the dirt. Just then, a raindrop splattered onto the note, leaving a round, dark mark on the white paper. She looked up to find that the previous clouds from this morning had molded together, turning gray and darkening the sky. Two more raindrops fell in rapid succession onto her nose and forehead. The other women, noticing the oncoming rain, quickly ascended the hill. Clair was reluctant to follow. Her feet felt stuck as if they, like her parents, were buried in the ground.

She was afraid to abandon what was left of them, to leave what little familiarity remained.

The rain increased and battered the thin parchment until it dissolved into the earth.

"Goodbye, *Maman, Papa*." She swallowed back a sob that lodged in her throat. She felt there was no more that could be said. With that, she turned and ascended the hill, leaving behind the last of her old life.

* * *

"*Mademoiselle! Mademoiselle!* Where are you?"

Clair snapped out of her thoughts and looked up from her pencil drawing to find a housemaid, dressed in the usual black garment and white apron, weaving around the dormant, leafless bushes in the private garden. The middle-aged woman strode along the path, her head swiveling back and forth. She stopped in her tracks when she spotted Clair sitting on a bench, a sketch book on her lap, facing a lifeless looking tree.

She approached Clair. "Here you are. Your aunt sent me to fetch you. There is a lady whom she wants you to meet."

"Me? Why me? Aunt Nicollette never wishes to see me, let alone have me meet with one of her guests."

The maid narrowed her eyes and put her hands on her hips. "I do not know, but she wishes an audience with you promptly." Her eyes widened. "Oh, my Lord! Why is your hair undone? It is unladylike to keep it down. It is also unsafe. If someone saw those curls–this is terrible!"

Clair touched one of her natural ringlets. Their multiple shades of silky, blond strands curled into spring-like locks. She had washed her hair and hid in the garden, where she allowed her curls to flow freely from their braided trap. The weather was unseasonably warm and sunny for winter, and her aunt's usual blatant disregard for Clair had made her think the day would be open to her own leisure.

"And look at your complexion! Your aunt will be furious

7

when she hears that you have been sitting out in the sun. Where are your gloves and parasol?"

Clair shrugged. "I had forgotten them."

The maid shook her head in dismay. "You constantly forget to protect your skin. It is already hard to keep yourself pale. Your poor aunt did not waste these past three years training you to be a genteel lady just for you to ruin it by destroying your complexion. Quickly, quickly! Come with me. I will make your hair presentable when we enter the kitchen. It will take a miracle to hide your curls before her guest departs."

The maid gestured in a sweeping motion for the young girl to hurry, but Clair did not budge right away. She tilted her face toward the radiant sunlight and relished the warmth for a moment longer. The maid tapped her foot impatiently, and Clair sighed and stood. She practically ran to keep alongside the maid as they entered through the kitchen at the side of the townhouse.

Once there, the maid grappled Clair's unruly hair into a smooth braid and twisted it into a bun at the nape of her neck. Then she practically shoved Clair the entire way to the front parlor room, which was covered from top to bottom in an array of pink floral decor. The room reeked of *potpourri*, and Clair was reluctant to enter because the overwhelming smell made her nauseated. She missed the simple aesthetics of her family's cottage.

Before she entered the room, an alarming, parrot-like voice speaking English with an American accent startled Clair.

"I tell you, thanks to your first Emperor Napoleon, there is a westward expansion in America. Manifest destiny, they're calling it. Many advertisements are promoting new beginnings and prosperous futures. Personally, I do not see the appeal. I am quite comfortable staying where I have been my entire life, in the settled commonwealth of Pennsylvania, and of course visiting Europe ever so often."

Clair's ears perked up when she heard the mention of America. She walked in right as the source of the screeching halted to take a sip of tea. Clair stood at the back of a distant chair, staring at the strange woman who seemed to be in her early 60s. Like a parrot, she had a large, round, beak-like nose. She also possessed piercing gray eyes and a strong chin. Her fashionable hairstyle carried an array of silver and gray strands. She wore a dark gray dress with a full skirt and long, puffy sleeves.

The stranger paid no mind to Clair's entrance and continued to speak across the room to Clair's aunt. "I've enjoyed my trip to Europe, but I long for my customized furniture and cuisine. You French have quite the skillful assembly of chefs but nothing compared to my personal cook. I am anxious to start my return trip home, but unfortunately, my traveling companion found a new employer and abandoned me. If only my Rodger were here to accompany me, God rest his soul."

Aunt Nicollette sat elegantly at the edge of the couch, her back straight and her hands delicately folded on her lap. She wore the most stylish dress with all of its trimmings to keep up with the other wealthy French women. She always kept an aristocratic air, both with company or in private. She took advantage of a brief pause in the woman's rant to raise her hand, beckoning Clair to come closer.

"Excuse the interruption," she said in English. "My niece just entered the room. Clair, this is Madame Glinda Marie Jackson from the Americas. She is an acquaintance I met at a charity ball the other night. Madame Jackson, this is my niece, Clair Annette Delacourt. She is my ward whom I took in after my brother and his wife passed away three years ago. She is the one I had recommended as your traveling companion."

Clair's jaw dropped. She had not been aware her aunt was making arrangements for her to travel to America. Upon seeing Clair's expression, though, her aunt gave a subtle warning scowl. Clair shut her mouth and turned her attention to Madame Jackson. She curtsied and said, "*C'est un plaisir de vous rencontrer.*"

Madame Jackson appraised her before she spoke in

English, "How old are you, girl?"

Clair hesitated to speak. Not used to being directly spoken to by people of the same status as her aunt, she feared she may fumble her words or speak out of turn. She stole a glance at her aunt, fearing her wrath no matter how small her potential mistake could be.

Before Clair was able to open her mouth to respond, Madame Jackson impatiently inquired to Aunt Nicollette, "Does she not understand English? I need someone who can converse with me fluently in my native language."

"Oh, she understands English better than myself," Clair's aunt answered, also in English. "Her mother was originally from the United States." She put her hand to her collar bone and cleared her throat to keep herself from saying more. Madame Jackson would definitely not take Clair if she knew from which part of America her mother originated. "Excuse me. Her mother spoke English, and I personally taught her proper elocution."

Madame Jackson waved her hand toward Clair. "Then what holds her tongue now? *Tu as perdu ta langue?*"

"She is shy. Clair, do not be rude. Answer her question and speak clearly so that she can hear you."

Clair swallowed a nervous lump in her throat. "I am eighteen years old, *madame*," she said in English.

Madame Jackson pursed her lips in contemplation and squinted. "Her appearance is unassuming. She doesn't possess a considerable amount of attractive features, though I would not consider her ugly either." She leaned forward to get a better look at Clair. "Her complexion is wanting."

Clair stole a glance at Aunt Nicollette, who was fidgeting with her gloved hands.

"It has been an unseasonably warm winter, and she often forgets to take her parasol and gloves when taking a turn about the gardens," her aunt answered. "Her father lived out in the country and cared not one whit about his daughter's appearance. It has been a struggle to rid her of this awful habit."

"It is definitely not a custom you should overlook when

traveling," Madame Jackson said. "The sun can be cruel overseas. Milky complexions are quite the fashion these days. Many young ladies take extraordinary measures to make their skin as light as can be. It would be an awful shame for her to become so dark no man will even think twice to court her. Has she come out in society yet?"

"My husband and I have only decided recently that she is ready to find a husband."

Clair shot a glance at her aunt. This was news to her.

"Is that why you wish for her to travel to America? To seek out a suitable husband?"

Clair stepped forward to interject, "I don't wish to burden myself with a husband."

"Do not speak out of turn, Clair," her aunt chastised.

Clair immediately dropped her gaze. "*Pardonnez-moi, madame.*"

Madame Jackson surprised them both by emitting a shrill titter. "Husbands are a burden, that is for sure." She wagged her finger at Clair. "But a necessary burden. You shouldn't dawdle when it comes to finding one, young lady. You should cherish your fleeting youth and use it to your advantage." Then she faced Clair's aunt. "However, I fear I do not have the time or patience to sponsor a young woman coming out in society."

"Oh, we would not dare ask that of you. I have a cousin who resides in Louisiana. He and his wife will take care of the matter once you are ready to relieve Clair Annett of her duties."

"Did you say her name was Clair Annett? As in clarinet, the instrument?"

Clair's aunt looked sheepish when she answered, "Her father loved music."

"Such a silly name, in my opinion." Madame Jackson looked over at Clair. "Do you enjoy music, girl?"

"*Oui, madame.* Very much so."

"Tell me, girl, who is your favorite composer?"

"I do not have a favorite composer. I enjoy the waltz, but I am also partial to hymns."

"You enjoy hymns, do you?"

"*Oui*. My father would play them on his violin every Sunday."

"I admire an appreciative ear to the Lord's music. Do you read the Bible?"

"I do." She averted her eyes. She had not read it since her parents were taken from her.

"I quite enjoy having the Bible read to me. My eyesight is not as good as it used to be, and I will need someone to read to me every day. Do you read other books?"

"*Oui, madame.*"

"What kind of books do you prefer?"

"I enjoy romance and mystery novels, but I prefer to read tales of adventure."

"Do you see traveling with me as an adventure?"

"*Oui, madame.*" Clair couldn't contain her enthusiasm. "Traveling to America is the best adventure one could have."

Madame Jackson straightened her posture and raised her chin. "I am proud of my country, and I would gladly boast of its beauty," she stated. "I am happy to hear there are those who are longing to see it for themselves." She appraised Clair once more. "You made quite the blunder earlier by speaking out of turn. I have no wish to travel with uncouth companions."

Clair's stomach hurt from anticipation.

"However," the old woman continued, "I do not have time to seek other options for an agreeable traveling companion, and your temperament seems amiable enough. You may practice your etiquette on the voyage. I will sail in a week." She turned her head to Clair's aunt. "Will she be ready to depart by then?"

Her aunt nodded. "We will have her things packed right away," she answered.

"Excellent. I will make preparations with the liner to prepare a room for her. All travel expenses will be taken care of by me, of course, and I will set an allowance for her." She slowly stood. "My knees are stiff from sitting too long. We can discuss details at a later time. I am tired, and I need to go home to rest.

Good day."

Her aunt stood and curtsied a farewell, and Clair followed suit as Madame Jackson passed them to exit the room. As soon as the old woman was out of sight, Clair spun on her heels to face her aunt, her eyes wide and mouth agape.

Her aunt remained poised and calm with her hands folded in front of her.

"*Je ne comprends pas, Tante,*" Clair said.

"English, Clair," her aunt interrupted. "You might as well get used to speaking in her language from now on."

Clair continued in English, "I don't understand, Aunt. I always thought you were ashamed of me, that you hid me from everyone so I would not embarrass you. Do you truly trust me enough to go out on my own? Did you know that it was my parents' dream for me to find a safe place to belong in America?"

Her aunt sighed and retook her seat on the couch. She patted the spot next to her. When Clair sat, her aunt twisted to speak to her face-to-face. "Your uncle and I may have been harsh with you these past three years, but we did it for your own good. When your father was disowned for disgracing our family by marrying your mother, I feared I would never see him again. I still regret not communicating with him after your grandparents passed and before he died. With no children of our own, I saw reforming you as a chance to right his wrongs. With your mother being what she was and you being ill-bred, we have done all we could to improve your civility. You have struggled to maintain our strict ways, and I thought you may do better with the lesser standards of America.

"My cousin has only one son, and he wishes to find a wife for him to start a family and pass down his business to his grandchildren. He is considering you as his son's bride. If he finds another woman to marry your cousin, he will either find you a suitor or give you work at his hotel once you arrive. I must instill in you how necessary it is that you take great lengths to continue this ruse, or you may lose any chance of finding a husband and making a way for yourself."

Clair looked down at her hands. Her parents never made her feel ashamed for her background, but her aunt always did everything she could to remind Clair that she held a detestable trait that must be hidden.

"I will gladly work for my cousin," replied Clair, "but I do not wish to marry until I find a place where I no longer have to lie about what I am."

"You willful and ungrateful child. It would be wise for you to heed my words. You will not likely succeed in your outlandish schemes, and if you do not take the opportunities your cousin and I offer you, you will find yourself lost and alone with no one to care for you. Do you wish to die on the streets?"

"I do not wish to die, but I long to find a home where I can be loved for what I am."

"You are a fool to think that any of us can be who we want to be."

Clair bit her lip and contemplated what she would say next. She could continue to argue and risk her aunt's wrath, or she could collect herself and keep playing the game until she found a chance to escape.

"What you say is wise. *Merci beaucoup.* . . . Thank you, Aunt Nicollette. May God bless your generosity and diligence. I am sure my parents are looking down, grateful for all that you have done to help me."

Her aunt placed a hand on Clair's shoulder.

"Do not waste this opportunity, *ma jeune nièce.*"

Clair straightened her back and nodded. "I will not. I promise."

Chapter 2

The moment Clair could see the New York City harbor, she was assaulted by dread. When her mother spoke of America, she always described it as green, lush with trees and rolling hills, of deep valleys possessing wide, winding rivers and large, purple mountains. She would tell of deer frolicking through grassy plains and critters jumping from tree to tree during warm summer sunsets. Birds sang melodic songs while the people sang with them.

The land that shrouded Clair's vision contained no trees, no vegetation, and the only wildlife in view were seagulls screeching as they darted through the boats' masts, as well as rats scurrying along the deck. With it being winter at sea, the air contained no warmth at all. In the chilly morning of their arrival, Clair could almost see the mist from her breath freeze and fall to the deck.

Madame Jackson, who now insisted that Clair call her Madame Glinda, did not have to wait in line to depart the boat like the second- and third-class passengers. She was given a personal steward who made sure that she and Clair were directed immediately to their nearby warm carriage, their luggage following not far behind. The steward spoke to Clair as if she were an equal to Madame Glinda, which made her feel like an imposter. She preferred her humble place among the working class, like with her parents.

The ride through the city brought even more trepidation. All Clair saw for miles were gravelly dirt roads, modern brick buildings, and a few aged stone structures–nothing as old as the ancient structures in Paris. Within all the streets and buildings were masses of people trampling through mud and slush, dodging the slow-moving carriages. Young boys peddled newspapers and little girls sold silk flowers while older folk carted around fish, bread, cheese, and textiles to be sold.

Clair was overwhelmed by all the activity playing out before her. To her, it was like observing a colony of ants climbing over each other. Both Paris and New York City thronged with people, but Paris was larger and had more space between its buildings, more greenery, whereas New York City seemed so much noisier and crowded together. It felt as if all of life converged onto these muddy streets–everything happened in this condensed area–and nothing existed outside of them.

'Is all of America like this?' she asked herself. 'How will I find my safe haven among all these people?'

As the carriage continued through the city, the buildings became smaller, and the people became fewer. Eventually, as the large structures became houses and spread further and further apart, a few trees appeared among the mud and grass along the road. Then, almost suddenly, valleys filled with an array of trees spread before her, and the large city behind her was hidden by hills. The houses they passed rested on acres of farmland. Orchards and rolling, dormant fields spanned for miles on either side of the road. Clair felt more at ease; this scenery reminded her more of her childhood home.

She gazed upon the fields as the wind blew the trees from side to side, as if the bare branches were waving at her. Although the scenery appeared dismal during winter, Clair felt that a diverse American landscape had more to offer than she could witness in one day, in one season, and she longed to see more.

The next town they arrived at was significantly smaller than New York City but still quite large. There were older structures that contained large towers built with brick, stone cathedrals, and mansions. The pair rested for a few days at one of the boarding houses residing near a hot spring. While Madame Glinda took long baths, Clair strolled around the compound, enjoying her first steps in American snow.

She stayed in a similarly lavish room next to her mistress. Servants came to help her dress, and every meal placed before her was covered by a large, silver cloche removed by another's hand to reveal an exquisite meal. Clair thought back to her aunt, Nicollete, and how she never allowed Clair to partake in such luxuries. No matter how many years she was under her aunt's care, she was still considered an unbefitting subordinate and thus still took her meals in either a smaller dining room or the kitchen. Aunt Nicollette made sure Clair practiced servant skills along with her etiquette lessons just in case she could not succeed in finding a place in her aunt's society. Here, though, she had somehow earned that place without having to do anything more than be a respectable companion.

Within a week, they arrived at her mistress's home in Pennsylvania. During their travels, Madame Glinda lamented over her previous home–the mansion her husband built. When her husband passed on, her nephew inherited the estate, and he promptly transplanted her into a smaller abode in the center of town.

What the red brick townhouse lacked in size, however, it did not lack in grandeur. Although not as gaudy as her aunt's home, every room was classically furnished with just enough decorations to make it appear elegant and comfortable. Clair felt relieved when she didn't have to breathe in the overwhelming smell of perfume and potpourri. She feared she would not have survived one more day in suffocation.

Madame Glinda had agreed to let Clair stay in one of her guest rooms until she found a safe way to travel to Louisiana. Little did her mistress know, however, that Clair was scheming to avoid Louisiana at all costs.

Clair had heard many wonderful things about America throughout their travels. Fellow passengers would talk about their home state and boast about its abundant resources, beautiful weather, and kind people. One fellow passenger, however, only complained about Louisiana. A round, red-faced, middle-aged, bald man with a drawl in his accent would tell stories about how the air was so hot and humid, your clothes would stick to you. The hostile bugs were larger than your hand, and the locals were just as mean as the bugs. Clair already dreaded the idea of marrying her cousin, but after hearing about the horrors of the state itself, she resolved to avoid Louisiana altogether.

Not long after they arrived in Philadelphia, while sitting in the morning room, Madame Glinda was handed a pile of invitations to upcoming Christmas festivities.

Clair sat quietly in one of the matching mahogany armchairs, keeping herself busy with embroidering a pillowcase. The old woman sorted through the letters, throwing most of them aside. Halfway through the pile, she held up one that caught her attention. Stubbornly refusing to use her lorgnette, she squinted at the words.

"Good heavens!" she exclaimed in her shrieking voice. "I cannot believe what I am reading! My feckless grandnephew has somehow found a bride willing to marry him. God bless that poor girl. There will be an engagement party in their honor at the end of this week."

Clair nodded while keeping to her embroidery. She had discovered that once the woman started complaining, the only thing required of Clair was to nod and occasionally murmur in agreement.

While Madame Glinda's complaints shifted to other subjects, Clair missed most of it. Her foremost thoughts were too occupied with hashing out different ways she could successfully become independent.

Unfortunately, being a young, single woman made every idea she conjured seem impossible, if not dangerous. Frustration over her inability to hastily resolve her dilemma caused Clair's fingers to fumble on the stitches. She set down her embroidery atop a pile of newspapers, and a headline in bold letters caught her attention.

The title of the article read: "Women of the Manifest Destiny."

Clair, unsure whether to risk browsing the article, glanced up to find Madame Glinda, eyes closed, slightly slumped on her armchair. Her chin tucked into the folds of her neck as her chest moved rhythmically up and down. Clair must have missed the moment her mistress's incessant prattle turned into snoring.

She took this opportunity to read the full article. Its content encouraged females of every kind to join in the migration out West. It boasted of women making a way for themselves where they may not have been successful elsewhere. Some interviews showcased women traveling with their husbands, some with children. Other single women took their chances making the trek to find lonely men in search of wives, or to seek employment as teachers, seamstresses, cooks, boarding house attendants, and so on. Clair was surprised to read that some women ran their own businesses, though the article also stated that not all of their vocations were honorable.

Just the fact that employment was offered in abundance was enough to entice Clair to partake in the journey, but what caught her attention the most was it stating that women of any background were welcome out West.

Clair's chest felt lighter, as if her corset had been loosened. She felt a new hope as she resolved to find a wagon train and seek employment. That way, she could procure the independence she was hoping for and, in doing so, be one step closer to finding a place of belonging. From what she read in the article, she might not have to look far once she arrived at her destination. Maybe the people who lived on the other side of the United States were more open-minded and understanding. Because all kinds of individuals with unique backgrounds were traveling there, maybe she would find people in a similar situation to herself.

Clair knew it would take a while to send out and receive letters inquiring about a wagon train willing to allow her to accompany them. In hopes of staying as long as she could in Madame Glinda's care, Clair resolved to be on her best behavior.

She planned to give her undivided attention, read books aloud with gusto, and refine her etiquette. She also knew this meant she needed to accompany Madame Glinda to every social gathering, the first being her grandnephew's engagement party only a few days away.

Chapter 3

A large, gray mansion with maroon trimming filled Clair's vision the moment she stepped from the carriage. Candles encircled by strands of evergreen decorated every window. A single wreath adorned the open front door. As they passed through the threshold, Clair was struck by the house's warmth and elegant decorations. The grand foyer's crystal chandelier illuminated and bedazzled the room, causing the crystal champagne glasses and silver tableware to sparkle. Everything was polished and refined. Evergreen draped along the railings of the grand staircase, and boughs of holly hung from ribbons that embellished the flowing decorations. More wreaths adorned every wall in the large house. Melodic sounds from a nearby orchestra filled the room.

A footman helped to remove Madame Glinda's cloak and bonnet before Clair's. Madame Glinda's uncloaking revealed a gray, glossy, silk taffeta dress, accented with elaborate black jewelry. Clair's heart raced and her back stiffened as her own cloak slipped off of her shoulders. She was still not used to such treatment and felt out of place in such an elegant setting. Clair peered down at her own plain, hand-me-down, dull green dress she'd received from Madame Glinda. It did not possess the fashionable off-the-shoulder cuffs or fancy trimmings. Instead, it sported half-length, flowing sleeves trimmed with a small amount of lace. Besides the lace on the collar and sleeves, she did not have any jewelry or even a bow, nor had Madame Glinda loaned her any for the event.

The footman handed their outer garments to another servant before escorting Clair and Madame Glinda to a grand ballroom. There, well-mannered gentlemen and graceful ladies conversed in any space that wasn't occupied by dancers, who twirled in the center of the large room. The gentlemen wore their finest tuxedos while the ladies' dresses were covered in fine, delicate materials of smooth taffeta or silk and lace with crinoline hoops that filled out their skirts. The array of colors reminded Clair of a blooming garden, the layers of skirts twisting and expanding like rose petals with each turn.

Clair tried to keep her face downturned, hoping to hide her unsuitable nose and dark brown eyes. She didn't want to risk making eye contact with anyone, but the liveliness of the party piqued her curiosity. Although she couldn't keep from gawking, she remained poised and inconspicuous, hoping not to be seen for what she truly was.

She had spent hours preparing for the party, trying to hide as much as she could by braiding her hair as tight as possible so no loose, tiny ringlet would reveal itself. And though she wore long white gloves and a small amount of powder on any exposed skin, she worried that if anyone paid too close attention to her, they would surely question her heritage.

The application of makeup was a precarious balance. If her skin revealed itself between her gloves and sleeves, people would wonder how she could have a tan in the middle of winter. If anyone noticed her paint, they would see her as an immoral woman. Queen Victoria, herself, deemed face paint to be impolite, and the rest of society scoffed at those who visibly wore it.

After the footman escorted the ladies to the grand door, Madame Glinda took the lead into the ballroom. She strutted into the hall with her bird-like nose high in the air, Clair following behind her, then perched on one of the chairs that lined the back wall of the room. Madame Glinda barely looked around but kept her face tilted upward with a perpetual frown. The grandeur of the decorated ballroom did not seem to impress the wealthy old woman. Clair, on the other hand, forgetting not to gawk, gazed in wonder at the beauty surrounding her.

Gold leaf decals accented turquoise wallpaper, and thick gold pillars stood at every corner of the room. Clair had never entered such a large, open space before. Although there were many grand houses in Paris, Aunt Nicolette's house was small in comparison, and Clair had never entered other mansions.

At the far-left corner of the room, she noticed a small orchestra playing a waltz. Clair swallowed down sadness that welled in her throat. She could not help but reminisce about her father and his violin, the way he would close his eyes and sway to the music as he accompanied other musicians during village balls back home.

Her focus swept from the band to a mammoth-sized fireplace, the largest Clair had ever seen. To one side of that stood a long table full of refreshments; delicate cakes, cookies, jellies, and hard-to-find fruits like sliced oranges covered every surface. During her voyage here, she had heard people discuss acres and acres of orange groves in the southern and western regions of the United States, and she wondered if the fruit she saw now came from there. There were also delectable hors d'oeuvres such as shrimp, lobster, cheese, and pâtés[1] to put on crackers. A large, elegantly styled crystal bowl full of red punch sat at the center of it all.

It was then, as she eyed the cookies on the one far side of the table, that she noticed him. He was a tall young man, one of the more handsome in the room, with thick and wavy dark brown hair. He stood stark still and alone against the wall among the crowd of minglers. He seemed not to mind their indifference toward him, however; he was intent on staring at her.

The shock of his undiverted gaze took Clair's breath away. She could not decipher his emotion. His thick eyebrows were low, but his glare did not appear angered but placid. He did not smile, nor did he frown. He rarely blinked and never redirected his eyes.

She began to worry if he was scrutinizing her appearance, but she dismissed this notion because he was too far away to notice anything unusual about her. A blush immediately crawled up her cheeks, though. She wondered if his cause for staring was because he found her attractive. She looked around, trying to reassure herself that maybe his attention was on someone else but could not fully verify that. He did not seem to care that she, too, was staring at him. In fact, he did not waver from his glare, and she was growing agitated from his rudeness.

After what felt like an eternity, a petite and beautiful young lady with blond ringlets pinned up in a fashionable coiffure approached the strange gentleman. Her head barely reached his collar. She wore a pink satin dress with a big, hooped skirt and off-the-shoulder cuffs. She looked proud with her small, upturned nose and pointy chin. Without his notice, she placed her thin, delicate fingers atop his forearm. He seemed a bit startled by the touch. He lowered his head to listen as she spoke to him but kept his gaze toward Clair. After the blond girl finished speaking, he offered his left arm to her, and they began to slowly make their way through the crowd.

Subsequently, the walk forced him to look away, which gave Clair a chance to inhale, only then realizing she'd been holding her breath. He seemed to lose interest in her. In fact, his distant look and unamused expression made it seem as if he had no interest in anything at all.

He walked slowly alongside the woman, who looked to be around the same age as Clair. The couple seemed to have an air of contempt for the crowd, and the woman's face showed annoyance as they trekked to the other side of the room. They occasionally bumped into guests without once stopping to apologize. As another woman walked across their path, they narrowly missed her because they didn't slow to let her pass.

Disgusted, Clair decided the "well-to-do" couple was not worth her time. Before she could divert her attention, though, an older gentleman approached the pair and gestured for them to follow. He had the same likeness as the younger gentleman but with gray strands highlighting his hair and a full beard. Clair was surprised to find them walking straight toward her.

She shifted uncomfortably, and Madame Glinda moved her judgmental gaze from the dancers to their arriving company.

"Nephew!" Madame Glinda screeched. "How nice of you to take time out of your merriment to greet an old lady such as myself. I'm sure you are very busy, what with hosting this grand party, and all. I feel so honored to be graced by your presence."

The older gentleman leaned toward his aunt to kiss her cheek. "My dear Aunt, of course we would come to greet you. You are, after all, an honored guest of ours. We wouldn't dare overlook someone as prominent in society as yourself."

Madame Glinda nodded in agreement. She then noticed the blonde, who stood poised and quiet next to the young gentleman.

"George," she said, "will you not introduce me to this fine young woman who takes the arm of my grandnephew?"

"Aunt Glinda," Mr. Jackson answered, "allow me to introduce to you Miss Catherine Elizabeth Cunningham from the Philadelphia Cunninghams. She is an accomplished young lady who also happens to be betrothed to my dear son Geoffrey. Miss Cunningham, this is my aunt, Mrs. Glinda Jackson. She has recently returned from a trip to Europe."

The petite girl, a product of genteel society, kept to her training and smiled politely as she gave a little curtsy. "Good evening. It is a pleasure to meet you."

That is when the older gentleman turned toward Clair.

"Will you not introduce us to your young companion, my dear Aunt?"

Everyone looked at Clair as if just noticing her for the first time–everyone, that is, except the quiet young man who kept to himself in the back of the group. She suddenly felt uncertain and lowered her gaze to the hardwood floor. Her Aunt Nicolette had gone to great lengths to teach Clair upper-class manners to hide her "undignified" past. Clair was careful with her elocution, though she could not completely hide her accent. She worried any blunder would showcase her actual background.

"Oh!" Madame Glinda spoke first with a wave of her

hand. "Clair, this is my nephew George Franklin Jackson and his youngest son, Geoffrey Benjamin Jackson. This is my traveling companion, Miss Clair Annette Delacourt. She has been with me since my trip back from Paris. Come, girl, and say hello."

Clair willed herself to look at the group. "*Bonsoir*," she said. "It is a pleasure to meet you. It was gracious of you to welcome me into your *magnifique* home. *Merci*."

Everyone nodded in reply, not wasting their time conversing with the "slightly" lower-classed French companion. Once she spoke, though, the young man's face angled in her direction. Again, he stared at her, his head tilted as if he were intrigued by her words.

Madame Glinda seemed bored of the formal introductions, however, and turned her attention to Miss Catherine.

"Young lady, don't you enjoy dancing?"

Miss Catherine hesitated. She looked at her fiancé and then back at Madame Glinda. "I'm afraid, Mrs. Jackson, that my partner is not in. . ." she cleared her throat, ". . .good form to dance."

The old woman leaned her head forward and shouted, "What did you say? I am hard of hearing!"

Miss Catherine's cheeks turned pinker as she repeated herself a little more loudly.

Madame Glinda grunted in agreement. "So true!" she exclaimed.

Clair was confused by this exchange. Mr. Geoffrey Jackson seemed able-bodied enough. In fact, as Clair's gaze surreptitiously swept over him, he looked to be in fine form.

"Young lady!" Madame Glinda continued, "you should dance with my nephew George. He may be older in years, but he still knows how to dance. Go, and I will keep watch of Geoffrey."

Miss Catherine's eyes brightened at the suggestion. She gladly took the older man's arm as he walked her to the dance floor for a waltz. The younger Mr. Jackson, however, stood silently where he was.

Clair watched the dancers with envy. Being Madame Glinda's companion meant that Clair was unavailable to participate in the festivities. It was a pity, for she truly loved to dance. This made her miss her father and mother all the more, for they also loved dancing. Her melancholy thoughts were interrupted, however, by her shrewd mistress's voice.

"Grandnephew, it is good that you have found a woman who is willing to marry you. I am astounded that anyone would consider you a useful companion. I have heard of her family, and they are quite the prominent members in society. She must have lacked good prospects to consider marrying you. I insist you not hesitate with setting a wedding date soon."

As he looked past the old woman's head, Mr. Geoffrey Jackson betrayed his annoyance by clenching his jaw while maintaining an otherwise neutral expression. Clair could feel the tension in the air.

After a period of uncomfortable silence, the younger Mr. Jackson cleared his throat and said softly, "The room is quite warm, and I am thirsty. I think I will get myself some punch. Anyone else care for refreshments?"

Madame Glinda gasped. "Heavens, no! Geoffrey, you should not be crossing the crowded room by yourself. Let Clair get us some punch while you sit here with me. Clair, surely you can fulfill that task."

"*Oui, madame,*" Clair replied dutifully as she stood. She managed to take a step toward the table before she was interrupted by Mr. Geoffrey Jackson.

"I fear I need to walk about and stretch my legs," he announced. "I am sure it is only a few paces away."

"If you walked on your own, you would surely bump into someone and make a scene!" interrupted Madame Glinda. She shook her head in dismay. "What a pity, Grandnephew, that your blindness limits your abilities to do the simplest tasks. I simply will not allow you to walk aimlessly and risk injuring your guests."

Clair was taken aback by this revelation. She felt silly

for not noticing it sooner and silently scolded herself for being oblivious to the signs. 'Shouldn't his careless stride and his distant gaze have been evident enough?' she thought.

The young Mr. Jackson swallowed before speaking again. He tried to hide his agitation, but his words came out strained. "Because you don't see it fit for me to go alone, allow me to escort your companion to the table. That way we can help each other carry the refreshments back."

The old woman contemplated his request before turning toward Clair. "I am quite thirsty. Clair, escort my nephew and get the drinks. Take care he does not trample over anyone on the way."

"*Oui, madame,*" Clair answered with a small curtsy.

As she turned to face Mr. Geoffrey Jackson, she found that his left arm was already extended for her benefit. She hesitated to take it, though. She still saw herself as a French peasant rather than a lady; a gentleman offering his arm felt unorthodox to her.

"Come, girl, take his arm so you can lead him!" Madame Glinda snapped.

Clair, startled by the sudden outburst, placed her hand near the crook of his elbow. However, she was unsure how to proceed. She had no idea how to lead a blind man through a crowded ballroom. She feared she would knock him into a chair or bystander and make a spectacle of them both.

He leaned close to her and said, "If you would be so kind as to guide me in the direction of the refreshment table, Miss Delacourt." His breath brushed her cheek as he spoke. His voice was soft and cordial.

She pointed toward the table before realizing how improper and futile the gesture was. She was glad he couldn't see her blunder. Unfortunately, someone else noticed her mistake.

"He cannot see you, Clair. You need to speak to him!" cried Madame Glinda.

Clair stifled a groan of embarrassment. "The table is to your right, *monsieur*, near the *grande cheminée.*"

However, instead of stepping in that direction, Mr.

Jackson surprised her by pivoting toward the wall behind them. She was too confused to correct him, and before she could muster a sound, he stretched out his hand and reached for the wall. Then, keeping his fingertips pressed against the glamorous wallpaper as a guide, he ushered them around the crowd. He walked with confidence and clearly did not need her help to find his way around.

He broke the moment of silence by speaking first. "If you don't mind my saying so, you have a lovely accent," he said. She looked up to see his radiant green eyes pointed in her direction. Seeing them so close, she was immediately engrossed in their beauty. Multiple shades of green mixed with gold flecks that highlighted the inner iris. There was no tell-tale sign that he was blind. She remembered seeing a blind man once who had bluish-gray discolored pupils. Mr. Geoffrey Jackson's pupils did not look discolored nor did his eyes wander around aimlessly. In fact, he seemed to keep them focused on one spot and usually toward whoever was speaking.

His right eyebrow shot up. "Do you not speak much, Miss Delacourt?" he asked.

In her ruminations, she had almost forgotten that he'd spoken to her.

"Oh! I. . . ." she faltered with her words as they got caught in her throat.

She didn't know how to reply to his compliment. The fact that he was paying particular attention to her accent made her feel all the more insecure. If he'd heard her mother's accent from her, or if she'd spoken with poor elocution, he would be able to tell she was an impostor. And if he could, then he may tell other people, and her reputation would be ruined. She would be kicked out of Madame Glinda's house, and she would be denied the money she was owed for her services. Her heart rate quickened at that train of thought, and her throat felt constricted.

Before she could dwell on those facts any longer, they stumbled upon a crowd of people blocking their path to the refreshment table. Clair was about to gently pull on Mr. Jackson's arm to stop their walk but found she didn't need to do that. He must have heard the group chatting and stopped himself. They stood there, waiting for the wall of people to disperse.

"Cat got your tongue, *mademoiselle*?" he asked with a quizzical brow. A playful, lopsided smile spread across his face.

Somehow in that moment, that smile was comforting. It slowed her heartbeat, and she could feel the pressure loosen in her airway. She replied cautiously, "*Pardonnez-moi*. . . . Forgive me, *monsieur*. I never know what to say when in the company of an aristocrat such as yourself."

He chuckled. "Do not think of me as equal to that of a gentleman! To these people, I am no better than a worthless rodent. My family and peers only see me as a feeble, pitiable creature whose only purpose in life is to be avoided at all costs."

Clair was shocked by his reply and stammered an apology. "*P-Pardonnez-moi, monsieur*. I am sorry. I didn't mean to offend. . . ."

He sighed. "It is not you who has offended, but I. I should not have spoken so openly to a cordial stranger such as yourself. Also, you apologize far too often. I propose that, if you agree to stop apologizing every time you speak, I will automatically forgive you of your endless faults." He smiled mischievously, and she covered her mouth to stifle a chuckle.

Encouraged by her muffled laughter, his smile grew. "Shall we be on good terms, then?" He held out his free hand and continued, "Let's agree, from here on out, to speak to each other as equals. I find class etiquette to be cumbersome and unnecessary."

Clair nodded and again felt silly when she realized he couldn't see her. "*D'accord*, I agree," she said and shook his hand. His smile and sense of humor disarmed her. No one outside of her family and village cared to partake in anything other than monotonous and stiff conversation. For the first time since she had arrived at the party–no, since she had gotten on the ship to sail to America–she began to feel at ease. He lacked elegance, which made her feel less inclined to be on her best behavior.

After their exchange, Clair noticed that the crowd had not yet dissipated. "The table is very crowded, *monsieur*; shall I get us the punch?" she asked.

He squared his shoulders. "If it's alright with you," he said, "I would like to get the drinks myself. If you can be so kind as to stay right here against the wall, I will be right back."

Gently extricating her arm from his, he followed the wall around the multitude of people. He skillfully weaved toward the table and then brushed his hand over the white tablecloth until he felt the glass punch bowl. There, a dark-skinned male servant ladled and distributed drinks. He happily gave Mr. Geoffrey Jackson two shallow glasses of the red concoction. Before Mr. Jackson left, though, he leaned over to say something to the servant. His remark must have been amusing because the man replied with a large grin. Clair was surprised to see that a wealthy gentleman like Mr. Geoffrey Jackson would take the time to chat with an employee. He seemed almost chummy with the man.

When Mr. Jackson returned, with impressively not a drop spilled, he stopped only a few inches from her. Instead of handing her the cup of punch, however, he seemed to be waiting for something. It took another heartbeat for Clair to realize that she needed to announce her presence.

"*Merci beaucoup*," she said and took a cup from his hand.

He smiled and lifted his cup for a toast. "To a new friendship," he said.

She couldn't help but return the smile and tap her cup against his. After they both took a sip, he said, "If it's alright with you, Miss Delacourt, I would like to enjoy my drink alone with you before we return to my aunt. She can be overbearing at times, as I am sure you have already experienced, given her arrogant attitude and prideful behavior. If I may be so bold, I am guessing your constant apologies are a symptom of having spent too much time with her."

Clair looked around for fear someone might have overheard his rude remarks. Not wanting to jeopardize her position, she chose her words carefully. "She can be a little strict at times, but *Madame* is also a *trés généreuse.* If it were not for her, I would still be in Paris with *ma tante.* I would have never had another opportunity to fulfill my dream of traveling to America. *Tout est bien qui finit bien.* All's well that ends well, my father would say."

Mr. Geoffrey Jackson took this opportunity of her mentioning Paris to inquire about her accent.

"Were you born in France, Miss Delacourt? I find your accent very fascinating. I quite enjoy immersing myself in the art of language. My lack of sight has given me the opportunity to focus on how people speak. It is a sport of mine to pinpoint the origins of an individual's dialect. I have tried to unravel your accent, Miss Delacourt, but it has a uniqueness to it. I can't quite figure out what other heritage you possess."

Clair stiffened. His discovery of her exact uniqueness was the last thing she needed. 'Will he soon figure out my secret?' she worried.

At her silence, Mr. Jackson's smile dropped into a frown and his brows furrowed. "I hope I did not say anything out of turn," he said. "My curiosity can get the better of me sometimes."

Clair did not want him to become suspicious, so she explained with a half-truth. "My mother was from America, and she moved to France when she married my father."

He seemed to accept the answer. "Ah, that would make perfect sense. Are your parents still residing in France?"

"No. . . ." she answered. Her gaze fell to the floor. Her chest tightened with sadness. "No, they have both passed on."

Mr. Geoffrey Jackson's face fell even more in sympathy, and he lowered his head in solemn respect. "I am sorry for your loss. I, too, know the hardship of losing a parent. I was ten when my mother passed on. But tell me," he continued before she could say anything about the subject, "how did you come to work for my grandaunt?"

Clair was not used to all the direct questions. Most people in high society filled their conversations with circumspection and vague words. She hesitated to say more for fear of revealing her secret.

"When my parents passed away," she said finally, "my aunt, who lives in Paris, took me in. She was the one who recommended me to your grandaunt, who was searching for a companion for her return trip to America."

Mr. Jackson shook his head in awe. "Miss Delacourt, you amaze me. My aunt is not easily appeased. You must possess an exuberant amount of patience and grace to still be in her company. I admire you for that."

Clair, stunned by his blunt remark, felt unsure of how to respond. She was not used to compliments, especially coming from a man. 'Is he trying to woo me? No, of course not,' she thought. After all, he was engaged. Still, she had heard of men pursuing other women even when already tied to someone. He seemed like a morally straight man, but how could she know for sure? She had only met him this evening. 'He does seem to be spending too much time throwing all his attention on me during his own engagement party.' This realization made Clair all the more uncomfortable. She could not risk calling attention to herself by seeming to flirt with an engaged man at his own party. She had to figure out a way to end their conversation before anything got out of hand.

Chapter 4

Miss Delacourt's dress rustled as she moved, her layers of crinoline rubbing against her outer skirts. Geoffrey could tell she was nervously shifting her weight. This sound and her lack of reply told him that his compliments, once again, could have made her uncomfortable. He wanted to place a hand on her cheek and feel for the rising heat of a blush, but he knew that to do so would be untoward. His direct questions and blunt comments were improper enough, but he found it easy to let his guard down around this girl. Most of his days were filled with silence while he secluded himself in the dusty, abandoned morning room at the back of the large house. When he was required to interact with other people of the same rank, he usually stayed hidden in the corner of the room and never spoke. He wondered if his comfort with her was because she was from a lower class. Most of the people he was close with were servants who worked for his father. He felt more at ease in a kitchen, surrounded by staff, than in a crowded ballroom. Not that she was a servant, but she held an air of humility that he admired.

Maybe it was her welcoming personality that made him feel at ease. She definitely wasn't like any of the snobbish, well-to-do women he had met before. He didn't appreciate those arrogant princesses who filled the room with their potent perfumes and obnoxious laughter. Could it be that in the small amount of time they'd spent together, she'd shown him more respect than even his family ever did? He wished for time to slow down so that he could learn more about this fascinating young woman.

Before he could say anything, though, she spoke. "Your

aunt is looking anxiously around the room for us. I fear we stalled for far too long."

Her voice changed with those few brief lines. Suddenly, it rang strong like a hand bell, but also kind and soft-tempered. He enjoyed her unique way of speaking. He could clearly hear her French origins in her accent, but there was also something else that was unique about her.

"*Monsieur*, don't you think it best we return to your aunt?" she asked again. "I fear she is *très agitée*."

He was so preoccupied with his thoughts that he'd forgotten she'd spoken. Despite being disappointed that their private conversation would soon come to an end, he repressed his emotions and smiled.

"Yes, of course," he said. "I am sure she is nearly close to death from thirst by now." Miss Delacourt suppressed a giggle, which made his chest fill with warmth. He went back to the table and replaced his empty cup with a full one for his aunt. When he came back to the spot he'd left Miss Delacourt, he offered his arm to her, and she gracefully took it. They walked on, always keeping to the wall.

He cleared his throat. "It sounds quite crowded. Are there many people dancing tonight?"

"Oh, *oui, monsieur*. Almost half the people are dancing a waltz at the moment. The other half travel between all the open rooms. The drawing room in particular seems to be popular."

"I am surprised you are not out there dancing, as well. Surely a young woman such as yourself can have any pick of eligible gentlemen."

'Unless she is betrothed to another,' he thought and fought a sudden urge to touch her hand where a ring would reside. He did not dare act on his childish curiosity.

"It would be a joy to participate in the festivities, but I am strictly here as my mistress's companion. . . ."

He could hear the disappointment in her voice. While they walked, he used this time to glean whatever information about her that he could. He guessed her height to reach his chin, though there was no way to tell for sure, unless he devised a ruse to somehow embrace her. From what he could tell, she had a healthy build. Her wrist, laying in the crook of his arm, did not feel like a twig nor did it feel like a tree trunk. He felt long fingers on the hand that rested on his arm and wondered if she knew how to play the piano. The occasional brush of her skirt against his leg suggested that her dress wasn't as full as the other women's, though the sound of the materials rubbing together did indicate that it was still made of a finer material than an everyday commoner's dress. It wasn't the distinct loud rustling sound of silk rubbing against the other fabrics of the skirt. He heard that kind of fabric donned by most wealthy ladies at balls. Miss Delacourt's dress sounded more like a whisper, as if there was no friction, like taffeta or satin. He appreciated a woman who did not overcompensate with extremely large hoop skirts. He grimaced at the thought of all the countless times he tripped over those ridiculous contraptions. He also noted her fragrance. She possessed an unfamiliar, subtle aroma of spring roses and exotic spices. He wondered about the origin of the scent because it did not smell of the typical French or English perfume.

As they neared the end of their silent walk, he could hear his aunt's loud and incessant chatter. She stopped as they came into her view.

"Ah! There you are! You finally returned," the old widow screeched. "Thank you, girl. I hope my grandnephew did not step on too many toes during your little stroll. He can be quite clumsy."

Geoffrey was appreciative of Miss Delacourt's lack of response.

"Grandnephew," his aunt continued, "I don't know why you insist on walking through crowded rooms. Your father already has enough to worry about, what with hosting this party and all. He doesn't need to worry about you bashing into all of the guests."

This comment gave the young man a fresh idea. He smiled politely in his aunt's direction. "You are absolutely right, my dear aunt." He spoke with as much charm as he could muster. "This celebration is quite overwhelming. It is exhausting to walk around, constantly running into people. I think I shall retire to my bedchambers now. However, I am not sure I will be able to find my own bedroom. I will need some help, but I fear all the servants are too busy with the party. Maybe Miss Cunningham, my dear fiancée, can help me to my room. Is she nearby?"

After he spoke, he held his breath, hoping the pious woman took the bait.

She gasped. "Oh, no! Nephew, have you no shame? It is not proper for you to be escorted to your room by your fiancée! Not only that, but with this being your engagement party, you should be here all evening by her side, doting on her the entire night. Insolent boy. Your ignorance of proper social decorum gives me a headache." She paused, and he wondered if she was rubbing at her temple like he often does when experiencing a headache. "I am torn between keeping you here to fulfill your duties as host or sending you away to decrease the risk of you embarrassing your family with your lack of scruples."

"I am sure my father would not mind me leaving early," he explained. "He knows how parties can be hard for me, what with so many people I must navigate around."

"Disabled or not, if you were my child, I would have you stay. However, you are not my child, and so I wash my hands of this. I will explain to your father and fiancée where you have gone." She paused again briefly. He could hear friction from her dress against the velvet padded chair as if she were twisting around in her seat. "I cannot see any servant with a free hand," she continued. "Your father should have hired extra staff for the party. Every servant seems to be too busy to help you to your room. I will have Clair escort you to the drawing room where there are less people and hopefully she can find the housekeeper to take you to your room. Clair, surely you can do this without causing a scandal. Once you are in the drawing room, you can ask around for a Negro servant named Minnie. Make sure you do not leave a public room together!" she added forcefully.

"Aunt, surely Miss Delacourt here is safe with me. What could a blind man possibly do to her?"

"You astonish me, Geoffrey. I don't know how you have not yet managed to single-handedly embarrass this family into obscurity. It is astounding how you have not learned by now the proper etiquette required of young gentlemen such as yourself. If you were my son, I would have surely thrown you into an institution where you would have learned how to care for yourself and how to mold into society."

This comment stabbed Geoffrey in the heart, but he maintained his composure. He clenched his jaw, trying his best not to show how much her words hurt him.

As an act of revenge, he purposely stumbled toward her and awkwardly pecked her forehead with a kiss. "My apologies. I meant to kiss you on the cheek. Good night, my dear aunt. I hope you enjoy the rest of your evening."

Her offensive remarks still stung, but he wouldn't let her hurtful words stifle his small victory. Geoffrey grabbed Miss Delacourt's hand and, with the same swift motion, placed her arm over his. He then led her toward the back wall of the room. His anger gave him a new kind of confidence as he walked her toward the edge of the familiar room and, using the wall, guided her to a door that connected the ballroom to a formal sitting room. She managed to keep pace, though with slightly unsteady footsteps. As they entered the much quieter drawing room, he took a deep breath. The music, barely muffled by the thin wall, played on.

He noticed he was still holding Miss Delacourt's hand, but he was reluctant to release her. The warmth of her palm radiated up his arm. It had been ages since he had felt soft fingers interconnect with his own. It reminded him of his mother when she would hold his tiny hand as they explored within the garden. His anger slowly melted away. After a few more breaths, he felt more at ease. He could hear a few people nearby chattering in their own private tête-à-tête. He quickly let go of her hand and took a step away from her. He hoped his ill-mannered behavior did not cause a spectacle and ruin Miss Delacourt's reputation.

She interrupted his train of thought. "I will look for your servant Minnie."

She took a step toward the hallway, but Geoffrey's hand shot out to grab hers once more.

"No, wait!"

Her footsteps faltered as she paused. His heart increased its tempo. He realized he needed more time with her. The engagement was to be short, and he knew once he was married, he would not likely get another chance to spend time with Miss Delacourt. Even just one dance with her would make him content for the rest of his life. He considered taking Miss Delacourt back to the dance floor, but he knew his aunt would give him an earful if he returned after he fought so hard to leave. He then thought of asking her to dance in the drawing room, but it was full of chairs for guests to sit on and rest. He also wished for privacy away from judgmental eyes.

Then, he thought of the perfect room.

He had to quickly think of a way to have just a moment alone with Miss Delacourt without her becoming compromised. He considered pulling her through the hallway door and hoping that no one saw them, but that may make her feel unsafe. He could feign a tumble, and Miss Delacourt could help him to a chair. That may clear the room of party goers, or it may lure more spectators.

In a sudden burst of inspiration, an idea came to his mind, but he knew it would take a miracle to succeed.

He took a few steps in her direction. "Do you still have your drink in your hand?" he asked.

"I-I do, but. . . ."

Before she could say more, he stepped forward, knocking his upper torso into her arm that happened to be holding the drink in front of her. The force caused the cup to tip toward what he hoped was the front of her skirt. Sure enough, what was left of her drink splashed across her body, and the glorious sound of dripping fluid filled his ears.

A startled squeal escaped her lips as she stumbled backward. All the guests in the sitting room halted their conversations, presumably to witness the commotion. Just then, a newly hired servant girl jumped into action. Although he had only met her once before, Geoffrey recognized the young former slave's soprano voice as that which belonged to Penny.

"Oh, goodness, Mr. Jackson, you done made a mess of this poor girl's dress."

He dramatically pressed his hand to his chest. "Oh, my, I am so embarrassed. We should escort the poor lady out of the room to give her some privacy."

At that, Penny jumped into action. "Here, miss, allow me to get y'all cleaned up."

The young angel in disguise then led Miss Delacourt into the back passageway that the servants used to travel between the kitchen, dining hall, and other rooms. The corridor also connected to a small, insignificant room that happened to be his favorite retreat and the very room that he had wanted to take her to for privacy. When the two women paused just a few feet past the entrance to the hallway, Geoffrey purposely bumped into both of them.

"There is so little room in here," he said with as much authority as he could muster. "The room down the hall would probably be a better fit for Miss Delacourt to fix her dress."

"Sir, do you mean that old, dusty morning room? I hear no one goes in there. Maybe we can take her to the washroom. . . ."

"I would hate to cause a scene," Miss[2] Clair Delacourt interjected.

Geoffrey jerked his ear toward the direction of her voice. Was she aware of his plan, or did she truly not want to embarrass them both?

Penny continued to fuss. She must have reached into a linen closet because Geoffrey heard the soft click of a small latch fit back in place. "Here's a towel for you," she said. "Oh, goodness, it's dripping all over the floor."

Geoffrey heard both women retreat further down the

hall, and he discreetly followed.

Suddenly, and unintentionally this time, he collided with a malleable wall of crinoline and fabric.

"Why have we stopped?" he asked.

"It is quite dark in here," Miss Delacourt answered with an uncertain ring in her tone.

"You stay right here. I will grab a candle," Penny said as she retreated. A moment later, she returned. "It's not much, but I will get another candle when I come back with some starch and a rag. I'll be right back."

Her footsteps disappeared through the doorway, which, Geoffrey noted, she left open. In a matter of mere seconds, the receding patter of those footsteps quieted, and it was just Geoffrey and Miss Delacourt in the center of the room. Her quiet breathing and the hush of her skirts against the floor suggested that she was turning from side to side in front of him.

"*Où sommes-nous*? Where are we?" she asked.

"We are in the morning room," he said. "This was once my mother's favorite room in the house. This is where she taught me to navigate without my sight."

"No one utilizes the room?"

"My father never remarried after my mother's passing. No one feels comfortable using the room. They prefer the parlor in the front of the house. I guess it's too painful for them. It's as if her ghost haunts this section. For me, this is the only room where I can be myself. I often come here to be alone. It is my little refuge, my sanctuary where I can hide from my family." He took a deep breath and squared his shoulders for courage. "I realize this is quite an unusual form of conduct, and if you are uncomfortable in any way, I can leave the room. But if you would just grant me this one favor, I would very much like to ask you to dance."

There was a moment of stillness. He could almost hear her thoughts whizzing through the silence.

"*Pardonnez-moi*, but I didn't know you could dance."

She did not sound nervous or upset by his conduct even

though he had just made an unusual request. And he hadn't realized he had been holding his breath until it came out in a rush. He chuckled a little and smiled.

"What did I say about apologies? My family thinks me too clumsy to dance, but my mother taught me a few steps right before she died. I have practiced often with the servants when they have the time to do so. I would have asked you in the ballroom, but we both know how other people would react. They would clear the room for fear that we might step on their feet. I promise, no servant has complained of sore toes for quite some time now."

Miss Delacourt laughed at his comment, and Geoffrey followed suit. Their merriment echoed in the empty room. When it subsided, he extended his left hand toward her and bowed playfully. His heart beat quickly as he waited for her response, then it nearly leapt out of his chest when her hand was suddenly in his. He gently pulled her closer and cupped his other hand around the small of her back.

He cleared his throat and whispered in her ear, "Do you trust me, Miss Delacourt?"

She chuckled again. "Good sir," she said with a teasing tone, "we barely just met, and you spilled a drink on my dress, but for some strange reason, I still trust you."

He gave her a mischievous smile. "Then I ask that you keep your eyes closed."

The music continued to play in the other room and could be heard easily where they stood. Without another word, and without knowing whether she complied with his wishes, he led her in their first waltz. There was no hesitation in her footing as she followed in step with him and the music. Although they kept an appropriate space between each other, he felt thrilled by her closeness. He could hear her breathing and feel the brush of her skirts against his shoes. Her posture remained perfect as he guided her across their makeshift dance floor. They went around and around, circling the entire empty space. She did not falter or stumble as he led her through a series of twists and twirls. Every time she returned to him, his breath caught in his throat.

Even though he couldn't see her, Geoffrey believed his dance partner was beautiful.

Chapter 5

Clair could hardly breathe. Every rhythmic step sent shock waves through her body, yet she resisted the urge to keep her steps small.

Her father taught her how to dance and how to trust her partner.

"It is a woman's gift to follow and a man's responsibility to lead," he would say. "You must allow yourself to blindly trust your dance partner."

It was never hard to trust her father. He had such a strong and confident presence, and he was a good dancer.

Mr. Geoffrey Jackson was also a highly competent dance partner. He confidently led her around the empty hardwood floor, her skirts sweeping along the surface. He seemed to know every corner of the room. She allowed herself to trust him as he led her in the waltz. The whole time they danced, her eyes remained shut, and she did not open them even when she feared they might stumble into a wall or when he twirled her around. His posture never wavered, and his steps never faltered. He used gentle cues to direct her where to turn and spin. When the music stopped, they followed suit. She opened her eyes and was stunned to find they were standing perfectly in the center of the room. It was as if they had not moved at all.

The two remained where they were, frozen in the same dancing stance and breathing heavily. She slowly raised her eyes toward him, illuminated by the moonlight streaming through the large bay windows. His broad chest rose and fell, and though his eyes were directed toward her, she could tell they were not completely focused on her own. She allowed her hand to trail down his shoulder to rest over his heart. It matched pace with her own, racing as he equally struggled to slow his breathing. His brow was low in contemplation.

Once their breathing evened, he released her other hand and brushed the tip of his finger on her warm cheek. It was a brief contact, but the sensation of his finger on her skin caused tingling to radiate across the side of her face. He cleared his throat and instantly dropped his hand while the other remained on the small of her back. Then his eyebrows shot up and he gave her a handsome smile.

In the heat of the moment, she took a step closer, shortening the respectable gap. He felt her motion and followed suit. They were mere inches from each other when the thud of a door shutting startled them both. The steady patter of shoes hitting the ground materialized and grew louder. Clair immediately backed a few paces away. Mr. Jackson frowned as he let go of her waist.

The footsteps came to a halt at the doorway.

"Minnie says vinegar will do the trick. She told me she wants to speak with you in the kitchen right away, Mr. Geoffery. I'll help this nice lady back to the drawing room once I finish fixing her dress."

Mr. Geoffrey Jaskson tried to suppress a smile, though in vain.

"Alright, I will be with her shortly," he said and turned in Clair's direction. "You're an excellent dance partner, Miss Delacourt." He gave her that big smile again and stepped forward, searching for her hand, which she graciously gave. He placed his free hand atop the one he was holding. "I hope there will be more chances to dance together again."

Clair frowned and sighed. "*J'en doute.* I doubt it, sir," she said. "Your aunt only arranged for me to stay on as her personal companion until I found a means to continue my journey on my own. She didn't want me to be traveling during the Christmas holiday. I plan on leaving town as soon as possible."

Mr. Jackson's shoulders drooped. "You don't mean to

travel during the harsh winter months?"

Clair shrugged and then realized he couldn't see her gesture. She explained matter-of-factly, "Your aunt only needed me to accompany her back to America as a traveling companion. I doubt she will wish to keep me longer than necessary."

Penny interrupted, "Come, miss. We need to fix that dress and get you back to the party. Mr. Geoffrey, Minnie will be cross with me if you don't go to the kitchen soon."

Mr. Geoffrey Jackson chuckled before squaring his shoulders. "Miss Delacourt, it has truly been a pleasure making your acquaintance. I only hope our paths will miraculously cross again someday." He gently led her hand to his mouth and grazed her knuckles with his lips. "I wish you good health and a safe trip."

A blush creeped up her cheeks. "*Merci, Monsieur* Jackson. *Adieu.*"

"*Au revoir,*" he replied, his wide smile unwavering.

Penny began to dab the pungent wet rag on Clair's dress as Mr. Jackson turned to leave. A realization struck Clair just as he was about to cross the threshold.

"*Monsieur*! Won't you need help finding the kitchen?"

He turned around. "No, thank you. I am perfectly capable of finding it. I know this house better than my great-grandfather who built it."

Without another word, he pivoted and left the dark room. After a few more dabs with the rag, Penny exclaimed, "I don't think there is much more I can do to fix this stain, miss. Let's get you back to the party now."

Clair peered down at the stain. The faded red blotch blended in with the dull green fabric, creating a muddy hue. Although it didn't look too conspicuous, it was still noticeable. Clair grimaced. She knew she was going to get an earful from Madame Glinda.

Penny led Clair through the dim service hallway, heading toward the lights, laughter, and chattering people. Music still played in the late hours of the night. Once Penny was able to safely and inconspicuously help Clair enter the sitting room, Clair relaxed her tense muscles. She leaned against a wall and placed a hand on her chest, breathing deeply to ease her racing thoughts. Although she had feared being caught alone with Mr. Geoffrey Jackson, she couldn't help but smile at all the details of their encounter.

"Clair!" a screeching voice bellowed. "That leaden-footed girl! Clair! Clair Annette! Where are you?"

Clair jumped and dazedly rushed toward the source of the call, nearly colliding with the older Mr. Jackson. The blonde girl from before clung to his arm. They both appeared to be inebriated; she giggled incessantly, and he stumbled around with his hair tousled. Clair decided it was best she avert her eyes and step aside from their path. She kept her head down as they passed. Miss Cunningham's droopy eyes recognized Clair and held up a white-gloved hand to her forehead in a sloppy salute. She pursed her lips and slurred, "Bon-jower." The awkward couple looked at each other and guffawed. Without another glance at Clair, they continued with their merriment.

Many guests showed the effects of a long night of drinking spirits. They laughed loudly as they staggered out the front door. Only a few people continued to dance and talk amongst themselves. Clair quickly retreated to the back of the ballroom where the old widow shifted unamused in her seat. Madame Glinda looked around erratically, her eyes squinting in disapproval. Clair took a deep breath and approached the old woman. When Madame Glinda spotted her, she instantly accosted Clair.

"Where have you been?" she demanded before her eyes widened as she registered Clair's skirt. "Good Lord! Your dress is ruined! So that's what took you so long to return. I wouldn't be surprised if you told me one of the drunken guests clumsily spilled on you."

Before Clair could think of a reply, Madame Glinda barreled on with her tirade.

"This party is starting to become a brothel," she

continued. "I told my nephew he should not be serving spirits during a Christmas party. I hope I live long enough to witness the day this city will put a ban on the Devil's water." She harrumphed. "He's a politician, for goodness' sakes! Or should I say *political lawyer*. He should be more careful."

She stuck her bird-like nose in the air and rose from her seat. "I am washing my hands of this mess," she said. "Come, girl! It's getting late, and I wish to go home. I am just glad I do not have to worry about you being drunk. What luck that I found a companion who disapproves of alcohol as much as myself."

Clair did not dare say anything to contradict her mistress. She did not like the feeling of drunkenness, so she never drank to excess. Her French upbringing, however, gave her an appreciative taste for wine. She silently followed the opinionated woman to the front entrance of the house. Their private carriage already stood waiting directly in front of the building, though Clair had seen Madame Glinda give no order to bring it around. She wondered how long ago her mistress had ordered for the carriage and worried her delay may bring on rebuke. As soon as they settled into the enclosed rig, the refined, well-bred woman slouched in her seat, her one arm draped across her belly while the other fanned her face.

"I have decided I am no longer attending these kinds of parties. They are too exhausting for an old lady such as myself. I would have left sooner if I didn't have to wait for your return. I should scold you for your tardiness, but I will forgive you. In truth, your absence gave me a chance to conjure up a plan to help my young, unfortunate relative." She stifled a yawn. "We will talk more about it in the morning. We are close to home now, and I am quite tired."

Madame Glinda's home was only a few blocks away, so the carriage ride was short. Although more in the center of town, the house was located on the same street as her nephew's magnificent home. When the carriage stopped, Clair followed her mistress up a short stoop and through the front entryway.

Clair was also tired, but the exhilaration from the evening

kept her in good spirits. When all her duties were done–such as reading the Bible and saying a prayer with Madame Glinda–she retired to her bedchamber.

Her small room was located on the second floor in the furthest corner of the house. It was sparsely decorated. Every wall sported yellow wallpaper with a white floral print design. The most colorful object in the room was a unique, multi-fabric quilt laying on the bed. The only other furniture was a stand with a washbasin, a trunk where she kept all her personal belongings, and a wooden chair next to a small window.

Clair dressed in her nightgown with only a flickering candle to illuminate the space around her. Once done, she lifted her green dress to study the stain. Its sleeves were frayed, and the lace was almost discolored from use. Wondering how to dispose of it, Clair turned her gaze to the quilt and remembered her mother sewing patches into its unique pattern.

"*Maman*," a five-year-old Clair inquired in her heavily accented English, for her mother preferred to speak in her native tongue, "is this the dress I wore when I was baptized?" She pointed to a white patch with her small, chubby finger.

"Yes, my sweet melody," her mother responded. "That's a piece of your baptismal dress. Now it's sewn in the quilt to tell more of our family's story."

"And that is *grand-mère's* dress!" Clair exclaimed as she pointed to a rough beige material.

"Mm-hmm, sure is," her mother replied as she focused on her work.

Then Clair pointed to a patch of slightly coarser fabric that was dyed purple and black in a zigzag pattern. "And that is the blanket you were born in."

"Yes. The medicine woman wrapped me in that blanket right after I was born."

"Will I ever get to meet that woman, *Maman*?"

"I hope so, baby. Your father and I'd love for you to see

49

where I was born one day."

"Why did you leave, *Maman*?"

Her mother had paused in her work, then, but didn't look at her daughter. Her eyes seemed to focus on a spot just beyond her work. A breath later, she blinked and resumed her task as if she had never stopped. "People took me and my mama away and made us live in a mean ol' place in another part of America," she said.

"Was it Papa?"

"No, silly. Your Papa saved me from that mean ol' place, and then he brought me here to France. We hoped we could find a safe haven here."

"Safe haven? Who is safe haven?"

Her mother stifled a giggle. "It's not a person but a place. It means . . . being somewhere you can be happy and not worry or get into trouble." She turned to grin at Clair. "Curling up warm in bed with your Papa and me on a rainy night is a safe haven. Sneaking into the neighbor's goat pen to pet the animals is not a safe haven."

Clair giggled. "The billy goat can hurt me with his horns!"

"That's right," her mother chuckled and poked little Clair. "So stop doing it!"

Clair squealed and jumped into her mother's arms.

They laughed together. After the merriment dissipated, Clair asked, "America was not a safe haven?"

"Your father and I were not safe to love each other," her mother answered more easily.

"Are you safe now?"

"We are safer here, but I hope one day we can go back to the people who helped me be born. There, we will be safe to love whoever we wish and be ourselves freely."

"With the people at the creek."

"Yes, sweet child."

"And I won't have to pretend you are Papa's maid in the market anymore!"

"With that group of people, you can let your hair down,

climb trees, and call me *Maman* anytime you like."

"I love climbing trees."

Her mother chuckled. "I know you do," she said as she put down her quilt and enclosed little Clair in a hug.

Clair blinked away her memories and reached for a pair of scissors. Cutting a few good squares off her gown, she then placed them in the trunk with the rest of her personal belongings. In her free time, she planned to add a few to her quilt. That way, she could remember the enjoyment she experienced this evening but leave it at that: a memory.

Satisfied with this solution, she crawled into bed with the music from the party still playing in her head. She was slightly saddened to think that she would never see the handsome, unique, young gentleman again but immediately shook her head at her trivial emotions. She would not let this slight misstep deter her from finding the life she had always dreamed about. She resolved to think of him no further and soon drifted off into a deep sleep.

Chapter 6

The next morning, Clair woke to the sounds of servants bustling about, getting ready for the day. They did not care to keep quiet because they were accustomed to Madame Glinda's heavy sleeping and apparent hearing loss. Clair flung the quilt away and stepped out of bed. After washing her face and twisting up her braid, she slipped into her day dress. It was the most cumbersome garment she had ever worn. The outer fabric was multiple shades of gray wool. She internally thanked the good Lord for cotton underdresses because it shielded her skin against the rough, itchy material. Like all the other dresses she was required to wear, this one was bolstered by a large hoop skirt, crinoline, and multiple petticoats. Connected to the V-shaped bodice, overtop her tightly woven corset, were long sleeves.

She ventured out the door, through the hall, and down the servants' stairwell. She smiled at a servant girl as they passed, but the girl only gave a courteous nod and stepped out of Clair's way. Clair longed to make acquaintances with the other employees, but they perceived her to be superior while everyone else in Madame Glinda's social circle regarded her as inferior.

To stave off the melancholy of isolation, she hummed a tune very similar to the waltz from last night. The music lightened her spirits almost immediately, and her footing was less weighty with each step. She was practically skipping by the time she made it to the morning room where her mistress preferred to eat their breakfast together. Parties exhausted Madame Glinda, and they arrived home fairly late, so Clair assumed she would still be asleep for hours. In the meantime, Clair planned to catch up on some reading before she was required to eat a late breakfast with her mistress. The anticipation of continuing her studies on covered wagons and the western expansion distracted her, and she at first did not notice someone else in the room. Yet there sat Madame Glinda in her pink, high-backed, overstuffed chair.

Shocked, Clair curtsied and stuttered, "G-Good morning, Madame Jackson."

The old woman only grumbled and waved for Clair to sit. They ate in silence, and, upon finishing, Madame Glinda delicately patted her napkin against the corner of her lips. She swiveled in her seat to face Clair.

"Are you prepared for your travels to Louisiana?"

Clair looked up from her almost empty plate. "I am nearly finished with all my sewing," she answered. "My new clothes will be more suitable for the warmer weather. I am told it can be quite humid in the summer."

Madame nodded. "I have heard the same thing. Do you have all the other necessary items? Hats, gloves, sturdy shoes?"

Clair, realizing this was turning into a full-length conversation, set down her fork and folded her hands in her lap.

"I was hoping to shop for those things once my allowance is allotted to me."

Madame Glinda lifted a finger in the air. "That is what I wanted to discuss with you. The amount your aunt and I agreed upon is formidable, but prices are rising, and I fear you may not have enough to cover all your expenses."

Clair nodded, though she had no idea where this conversation was going.

"I have a proposition for you," the widow continued. "I propose you stay here for a few more months. I am developing a project, and I will need your help in order to accomplish it."

Clair blinked. "How can I be of help?"

"My young, blind grandnephew, who you assisted yesterday, is soon to be wed to a prominent young lady. This marriage will expose him to the higher genteel crowd. He is, however, not accustomed to practicing the rules of etiquette that we are bound to follow. I believe he is in need of some tutoring. I think it unfair for his future wife to be shunned by society just because he is unable to conform to our standards. In absolutely no way should she have to carry such a heavy burden of shame.

"That is why I wish to volunteer you to help me in that matter. I would like to hire you as an etiquette tutor. You have a fresh knowledge of the matter, and you have shown much progress since the day I met you. I will, of course, increase your allowance, and you do not have to worry about rent. I insist you continue to reside here. That way we can continue eating our morning and evening meals together. His home is not far away, so you won't be burdened by a long commute.

"My grandnephew can be quite stubborn, but I have noticed that you are patient and sensible. I am confident you will make great strides with the task at hand. I am not sure how much he already knows about manners, but I am assuming it will be a big undertaking, and you will be generously compensated. I believe this will be a suitable arrangement, don't you think?"

Clair's eyes widened with every word from the widow's mouth. She did all she could to keep her jaw from dropping, stupefied by this new, unforeseen fork in her road. She had hoped to start her new life soon. She had sent letters inquiring about wagon trains that may allow a single woman to join. So far, most replies were in the negative except one where a widower offered passage if she considered marrying him first. Clair shuddered at the idea of marriage, let alone to a stranger. She was avoiding her cousin for that very reason. Her next plan was to seek employment at a hotel in a fort near the trailhead. There, she hoped to find a group who did not care that she was an unmarried woman.

She contemplated the idea of becoming a tutor. She had no idea what that kind of job entailed. She assumed it was similar to how her aunt taught her etiquette. Sitting in a chair instructing someone sounded easier than scrubbing floors or changing countless strangers' soiled bed sheets. On top of that, the guarantee of a salary outweighed the benefits of finding employment elsewhere. With no wagon trains mobilizing until spring, the idea of being hired as a tutor seemed reasonable as long as it lasted only a few months.

Clair cleared her throat. "What you say does sound reasonable," she replied tentatively. "I will accept your proposition."

The old lady clapped and nodded. "Excellent. I have already sent a note to George explaining my idea. He shouldn't have any reason to say no, though his son might object. That young valetudinary, however, has no say in the matter."

At that moment, a maid came in to take away their dishes. Clair and Madame Glinda discussed nothing more on that subject. Yet, as the pair continued their daily activities of reading and conversation, a realization hit Clair: She had been so busy worrying about her plans that she hadn't recognized she would be spending the next few months with Mr. Geoffrey Benjamin Jackson.

* * *

Geoffrey sat in his usual spot at the dining room table. To his right, his father's newspaper ruffled and shuffled. He detected the bold, acidic scent of coffee, and he heard the parlor door open with the clattering of dishes. The aroma of fried meats and eggs and the sugary scent of maple syrup overwhelmed his nose. Minnie, the head housekeeper and a former slave, positioned herself behind Geoffrey.

"I got your favorites today, Mr. Geoffrey!" she said in her robust southern accent. "Fried eggs, pancakes, and ham slices." The plate reverberated as she set it on the table in front of him. "I notice you been outta sorts lately," she continued, "so I planned a large brunch today. I hope this cheers you up."

Geoffrey turned to smile at her. "Thank you, Minnie. It smells absolutely delicious."

She patted him on the shoulder. "Child, you shouldn't flatter me so. You're looking pale. I hope you ain't gettin' sick." She placed the back of her hand on his forehead and mumbled, "You ain't got a fever. . . ."

"Minnie," his father chimed in, "you need to stop mothering him so. He is going to be a married man soon and needs to learn how to care for himself."

"Yessir, Master Jackson, you are absolutely right. I'm only keepin' him healthy for the weddin' day, that's all. That bein' said, if I don't see you, ch–I mean, Mr. Geoffrey, eat all of your breakfast. I'm gonna call the physician. So, you best be eatin' this good food. No one wants a doctor 'round."

Geoffrey forced another smile. "I'm fine, Minnie. I just have a lot on my mind right now."

That was only a half truth. One subject dominated his mind: the elegant young woman he had danced with the previous night. His mind raced with every detail of every moment he had spent with her. Ever since then, he dissected every conversation they shared. He thought about her kind nature and unassuming strength. He remembered her scent, the way her hand felt in his, and her beautiful voice with her unique accent. He longed to encounter her again and know her better, but she said it would not be so. This fact put a damper on his day.

His thoughts were interrupted by a sarcastic "mm-hmm" from Minnie.

"I'll leave you to eat your brunch, then," she said. "Your eggs are to the west, pancakes to the south, and ham to the east. Oh, I almost forgot; I placed an extra cup of syrup north of your plate. The utensils are where they always is." She lightly squeezed his shoulder before her footsteps receded into the kitchen.

He devoured his meal. It was not hard for him to find his appetite with the food smelling so delectable. No conversation interrupted his meal, either, because he and his father rarely spoke. Halfway through their quiet breakfast, however, the head butler entered.

"A note for you, sir," he said.

Geoffrey knew the uptight man was speaking only to his father because Geoffrey had no acquaintances outside of his home. He heard his father place the newspaper down.

"Ah, excellent. Thank you, Jeremiah. That was rather quick."

Familiar with his father's ways, Geoffrey knew the rustling he heard was the stationery being unfolded followed by a brief pause before it was refolded. But then his father startled him with a booming voice.

"Son, I have something of importance I need to speak with you. Your grandaunt wrote to me early this morning. She has brewed up a scheme that involves you. She mentioned your rude behavior last night and is fearful this will ruin the reputation of your future wife. She wishes to hire a tutor to educate you on proper etiquette."

Geoffrey lowered his head. "With all due respect, Father, I was not aware my leaving the party early to rest caused such displeasure."

"That is exactly why you need someone to teach you proper manners. The celebration was in your honor and in your home. You should have stayed until the very last guest departed. Not only that, but you had also spent most of your time either standing in the back of the room like a wallflower or conversing with that French servant."

"She was Aunt Glinda's companion."

"That is beside the point. That girl is below us and not worth your time. You should have accompanied your fiancée and greeted all of our esteemed guests."

Geoffrey scoffed. "Why bother conversing with people who do not feel comfortable interacting with a blind man? I wish you wouldn't have betrothed me to Miss Cunningham. What good could it possibly do?"

His father slammed the table. "What's done is done. You are engaged now, and with that you will be more closely watched by society. You are required to be diligent and present yourself as a respectable gentleman. I will not allow you to ruin Miss Cunningham and our family's reputations. Besides, I do not wish to refuse your aunt because she is personally funding this undertaking."

His tone then lowered. "I am expecting your full cooperation and will hear no further protest. Is that understood?"

Geoffrey could only nod in reply.

"Good. With any luck, this venture should only last a few weeks."

A searing heat radiated up Geoffrey's neck as he bit his tongue. He didn't need a tutor. He was taught proper etiquette from his mother and by a multitude of tutors after her death. He purposely chose not to utilize those lessons. His "poor" manners repelled people and allowed him freedom to do as he pleased.

Despite his ire, he kept his head down. Arguing would just lead to a sizable beating from his father when he least expected it. The man wasn't averse to wielding his belt despite Geoffrey's age.

While he silently ruminated on his displeasure, chair legs screeched against the floor, indicating that George Jackson had risen from his seat.

"Your aunt apparently already found you a tutor and wishes for us to meet this person today. Be ready for their arrival."

His footsteps receded out the door and down the hallway. Geoffrey's ears rang; they often did when he was under an unbearable amount of stress. He felt like someone had fastened a rope around him, and he couldn't move. He hated the way his father treated him like a child. He was a mature, grown man. Although he wasn't academically smart like his brother– how could he be when there were no books with raised lettering for him to read–he knew that he was capable of being more than an unwanted fixture in a home. He moved about the house without needing any guiding stick or assistance. He worked in the kitchen by chopping food, stirring ingredients, putting away washed dishes, peeling or pitting fresh produce, and other menial tasks. He aided Minnie with the polishing, folded linens, and weaved baskets. He could groom and dress himself. The list went on.

Sure, he kept his abilities a secret from his family. This was so they could leave him alone. He had hoped to live the rest of his life among his friends in the servants' quarters, isolated but of use. But it was all for naught because he was being forced into society by marrying a woman he hardly knew. Only once did he and his fiancée meet face-to-face, and that was an hour before the engagement party last night. She mostly ignored Geoffrey and concentrated her attention on his father.

He slammed his fists against the table. His tense muscles released just enough for him to leave his chair and, brooding, return to his dusty hiding spot in the corner of the house.

* * *

A mere two hours later, Terrance, a footman and one of Geoffrey's few confidants, escorted him to his father's study. Geoffrey trudged into the room, making sure that his countenance showed his displeasure. He cringed from his aunt's ear-splitting, shrill chatter as she expressed her displeasure of his conduct last night. Gradually, he found his way to the corner of the room where the bookshelves and right wall met. There, a small fireplace radiated heat against his legs. The sensation distracted him, and he didn't pay any mind to the conversation until his aunt squawked the word "chaperone." With intrigue, he tilted his head toward the conversation; he had assumed he was being tutored by a man. Only a woman tutor would require a chaperone.

"Minnie can chaperone them," his father replied. "Even though she is a Negro, she is competent and trustworthy."

"That will do, I suppose," mumbled his aunt.

"Excellent," George Jackson continued. "With that settled, I must be leaving. I apologize for the abrupt end to our conversation, but I have a meeting with an elected official today, and I cannot afford to be late. I will have Minnie show the new tutor around the house today so she knows where to conduct her lessons. We shall start on Monday. We look forward to working with you, Miss Delacourt."

At the mention of her name, Geoffrey's balance faltered. He caught himself before anyone could notice, though. Waves of emotions, from shock to elation to rage, surged through him.

Heavy footsteps exited the room, and the only noise Geoffrey could identify was the ringing that returned once more in his ear. 'Not only am I stuck being unnecessarily tutored on etiquette,' he thought, 'which is embarrassing enough as it is, but by Clair Annette Delacourt? I can only imagine what falsehoods were spoken to her to convince Miss Delacourt that I required her tutelage.'

"Good afternoon, everyone," Minnie greeted as she entered the room, interrupting his thoughts. "Mrs. Jackson, Master Jackson said your friend would like a tour of the house. Miss Delacourt, I presume? It's a pleasure to meet you. I'm Minnie, the head housekeeper."

"*Enchanté*," Miss Delacourt replied in her soft yet sure voice. "It is a pleasure to meet you."

Her words sent a lightning bolt through Geoffrey's chest. 'Why does she unhinge me so?' he thought. 'Could knowing someone for a mere few hours cause such a reaction?'

"Hey!" exclaimed Minnie. "A French girl! I'm from Louisiana, so I know a little French myself. *D'où venez-vous?*"

"I come from Paris, France."

"Well, ain't that sum'in. We may not be from the same country, but we are more alike than meets the eye."

For a moment, a stillness encompassed the room. Geoffrey, sensitive to this, could almost feel the silence.

Intrigued by this interaction, he had to ask, "You mean, because of your similar French tongue?"

A small pause, then Minnie answered cheerfully, "That probably be so. Now, let's have that tour!"

* * *

Clair could hardly sleep that night. It wasn't the stress of tutoring Mr. Jackson that kept her awake, though she did see it all as a strange turn of events. She was perplexed by the housekeeper's comment about being "alike." The woman gave her a meaningful look after those words were spoken. Clair couldn't decide if her comment was a threat, a warning, or if she was just pointing out their similar language. Clair also feared Madame Jackson would possibly hear the meaning behind the words. Although they brought up nothing about the subject after that, Clair was on edge the rest of the day.

The next morning, she tried to push her worries aside to prepare for her duties as a tutor. After breakfast, she searched for any brochure pertaining to proper etiquette that she may have kept from her voyage. Next, she wrote a list of manners that she could teach Mr. Geoffrey Jackson before prioritizing each subject. Once she had a general idea of a lesson plan, she layered herself in coats and scarves and walked the mile length through the brisk yet dry air to calm her nerves.

Once she arrived, she was directed into the parlor room. It was unusually large and sunny and thankfully did not possess the ugly bright colors she normally saw. Instead, the furniture was beige with pastel floral print. The walls were robin egg blue, and all the trimming was polished wood. Silk flowers sat in vases on end stands, and large green house plants, arranged by height, aligned the corners. She was surprised to find that Mr. Jackson had not yet arrived. She chose a set of chairs near a small table to begin their lesson and sat.

Self-doubt grew with each minute she waited. By the time a half hour passed, she no longer felt that being hired as a tutor was a good idea, and she contemplated leaving. Just as she was about to extricate herself from her seat, though, two men entered the room.

The first man had brown skin and wore the uniform of

61

a footman. Pacing behind him was the younger Mr. Jackson. He had the same sour look from the day before, only this time he did not walk with heavy footsteps. Instead, he rushed past the footman and threw himself on one of the overstuffed chairs. The footman cleared his throat, clearly displeased with Mr. Geoffrey Jackson's misconduct. When he did not respond to the servant's subtle cue, the footman explained.

"Miss Delacourt, Minnie will be in shortly. She was detained due to a mishap in the kitchen. I will be right outside the door if you require anything."

Once it was just Clair and Mr. Jackson in the room, there was a sudden discomfort. Being alone with him felt very different from the evening of the party. That night, he'd felt like a friend who'd just wanted to share companionship. Today, he seemed almost threatening with his brooding expression and dismissive posture. This convinced Clair all the more that the tutoring job was a bad venture.

Before she could convince herself to suffer a minute more of his mood, she jumped out of her seat and raced to the open door. Only a few more paces and she would be safely out of the room. However, before she could walk out the door, a large canvas painting hanging on the wall to her right caught her attention. It depicted a grove of trees. Her father's voice in her head halted her.

"You are a brave girl, my little clarinet." He had told her this after she'd fallen from a tree and skinned her knee. "You are not afraid to leap, and that will take you far. In life, you will have to take risks. Sometimes the branch will break, and other times you will be rewarded with a higher limb that will take you even further to the heavens. It may be scary, but do not give up. Keep climbing."

Clair wanted to give up so badly. She felt as if she had already pushed herself past her comfort zone too many times. How many more leaps did she have to take to avoid her cousin and find the land in her mother's stories? Was it worth it? Could she not feel accomplished just for making it to America?

She imagined being halfway up a tree with its branches stretching into the sky. She couldn't tell how many branches needed to be climbed before she reached the top nor how many more uncomfortable situations she had to endure in order to reach her goal.

Was it worth continuing? Should she just complete her time with Madame Glinda, find her cousin, marry, and live a life full of secrets and restraints? Would she regret stopping in the middle of her journey? To give up now could mean she would never know the feeling of freedom in her heart. She thought back to her father and what he would say.

"Do not give up," she heard again in her head. "Keep climbing."

With a new resolve, she whirled back to face the room. As she turned, Mr. Geoffrey Jackson was only a few steps from her, barreling toward the door. Before she could dodge him, they collided. Clair gasped as the unexpected force caused her to teeter backward against an end table. She prepared herself for the impact and subsequent fall, but Mr. Jackson took hold of her waist and braced against a nearby armchair with his other arm. He towered over her while she was nearly parallel to the ground.

She swallowed back her shock and gazed upon his face, which was only a few inches from hers. His eyebrows were knitted together in concern, his vibrant green eyes frantically moving about. Both panting, they stayed in that position for a moment, making sure to not disrupt their delicate balancing act. Eventually, his eyes steadied, and he gazed steadfastly ahead forward as if focusing on her . . . but not quite. He breathed deeply through his nose, pulled her fractionally closer, then pushed against the chair and righted them to a standing position. Once they both had solid footing, he shifted his hold to grab her shoulders.

"Are you alright?" he asked.

Not wanting to betray her emotions, she nodded and then closed her eyes in frustration.

He stepped back. "Did I just feel you nod?" he asked with a

quizzical brow. "Did you just nod at a blind man?" His lips curled into a crooked smile.

She stared at the floor, her cheeks warming. "Your movements are so fluid, *monsieur*. I constantly forget you cannot see."

"So, this is not the first time you have made this blunder?" He pressed his lips thin but continued to smile. The image was oddly comical.

She couldn't help joining. "Please," she said, trying to suppress a giggle, "I am too embarrassed."

He wiped his mouth as if to smear the grin away. After he regained his composure, he said, "I'm sorry. I shouldn't jest. You should not be embarrassed. It was I who acted like a fool and ran into you. I thought you were leaving, and I was trying to catch up to you. Come, sit, we have much to discuss."

He returned to the table, his arm slightly extended to find a chair. When he did, he pulled it out for her to sit. Only then did Clair notice the footman and Minnie with a tray in her hand, standing a few feet behind the entrance. Although the footman looked bewildered, Minnie seemed more amused.

"I see you two have started your lessons. How nice of you, Master Geoffrey, to offer this nice young lady a chair," Minnie said as she glided toward their small table and placed the tray upon it. "I'm glad someone is instilling some manners in this fusspot." She nudged Mr. Geoffrey Jackson's side with her elbow and winked at Clair. "I brought some refreshments. Make sure you don't let this young man eat it all his own self. I'll just be sewing in that chair over there; don't pay me no mind."

When they were all settled, Mr. Jackson spoke.

"I have been. . . . What I mean to say. . . . I apologize, Miss Delacourt, if I seemed agitated earlier. My aunt insists I have a tutor, and though I don't agree with her, I do have the highest respect for you. I understand that you tutoring me is a business transaction between you and my aunt. I would hate to deny you another source of income. For that reason only am I willing to be your most attentive student." With a twisted half grin, he rubbed his hands together. "So, what lesson did you have planned for me today?"

"Well," Clair said hesitantly, "I thought we could discuss table manners. That was one of the first lessons I was given."

"By all means," replied Mr. Geoffrey Jackson.

"I wanted to start with explaining how to offer a lady her chair, but you already know how to do that."

"Yes, I do." He chuckled. "I also know to have my napkin on my lap and not speak with my mouth full."

Clair, embarrassed by her ignorance, stammered. "O-Of course you would know that. We all were taught that as children." She blushed, unsure of what to do now. "I would not want to teach you manners you already know. . . ." She looked down at her hands, unsure of what to say next.

"How about you quiz me, and if I do not know an answer, then you can teach me that subject."

From there, the rest of the afternoon involved her asking a question, using the brochure as a guide, and him responding with the correct answer. After a while, she started to give him more difficult questions.

"Should an asparagus be cut with a knife or picked up with your fingers?"

"It is unbecoming to cut an asparagus," he answered in a mock official tone.
"It is better to eat it with your fingers."

"Is it proper for a man to call on a woman or a woman to call on a man?"

"A married woman may visit a man who is not her husband but not often for fear of scrutiny. If she is unmarried, a woman should never call on a man alone. Does this mean you are, or once were, married, Miss Delacourt? Seeing as you called on me without an escort."

"It is rude to ask such a direct question, *Monsieur* Jackson."

He scrunched up his nose. "*Was* it a direct question?" he asked with a lilt in his voice, "I only want to better understand the intricate roles of proper etiquette."

She blushed. "Very well, I will explain. Although I have never been married, I am a tutor, and so the rules do not apply as strictly. But to preserve our reputations, we have Minnie monitoring to ensure our interactions are proper."

He leaned back on his chair and folded his arms, his smile spreading.

"I knew that. I just wanted to see if you were ever married."

"*Monsieur* Jackson!" exclaimed Clair. "You are being *très effronté*! I cannot make sense of this situation. Your behavior seems abhorrent at times, yet you answer every etiquette question correctly. My tutelage is of no help to you."

"Please, if we are to be working together, I would prefer you call me Geoffrey."

"I am sure you know why that cannot be so. You are engaged to another woman, and I am your employee. It is improper for me to call you by your first name."

"Miss Delacourt, I have had tutors my entire life. As a blind boy, societal rules were a priority and pressed upon me with vigor so I wouldn't be an inconvenience to the able-bodied population. As I got older, no one treated me any better just because I had good manners, so I chose to follow my own rules. I still treat people who deserve it with respect, but I refuse to stress myself in following every frivolous rule just because high-class society deems it important."

"*Pardonnez-moi*, but I must be frank with you. Blind or not, you are, in fact, part of that high-class society. You are about to marry a woman who comes from a highly respected family. How will you continue to live the way you wish without disgracing everyone around you?"

"If it were up to me, I would live my days hidden in my little corner of the house, away from society."

"That seems like a lonely life."

"I am used to it."

Clair let his words sink in. "*Monsieur* Jackson, you clearly do not need a teacher."

He ducked his head and grimaced, almost like a dog waiting for rebuke.

"You need a friend."

His head shot up, and he smiled at her with almost hopeful exuberance.

She continued, "I have a proposal."

His eyebrows jumped, and he chortled. "Come now, Miss Delacourt. . . ." he teased, his flirtatious tone causing her to blush. "It is improper for a woman to propose to a man."

She smiled. "I mean a business proposition. We continue to meet, but I will act more as a personal liaison. We will tell your family that I am tutoring you, but instead of lessons, I can read you books. We can have discussions. If you need help writing letters or any other menial task, I can assist with those, as well. You can show your family your progression in good behavior, so we do not raise suspicion. *Avons-nous un accord*? Do we have a deal?"

"Miss Delacourt, you are slyer than you led us to believe. So, what you are saying is, we can be secret friends? Does this mean I can call you by your first name?"

"*Non.*"

"What if it started with a 'Miss?' Surely 'Miss Delacourt' is quite a mouthful. Heaven forbid you require '*Mademoiselle.*'"

She leaned back and took a moment to contemplate. "I will allow it but only when we are in session. Outside of this room, we can only call each other by our formal names."

"Does that mean you will call me Mr. Geoffrey?"

She couldn't help but roll her eyes. "If you insist."

"Well, then, Miss Clair, we have a deal."

He extended his hand for an official handshake. Even with it being semi-formal, hearing her first name spoken aloud by him made her stomach flutter. She suppressed a giggle as they shook hands.

Feeling lighter, now that she obtained a job that was more to her liking, she asked half-jokingly, "What shall we do to fill the time today, *Monsieur* Geoffrey?"

He paused for only a moment before answering, "There is a gentleman who knew the late Mr. Louis Braille. Do you know any of Mr. Brialle's work?"

"That is a French name, but I only faintly recollect hearing of a Louis Braille."

"He is a Frenchman who became blind at a young age. As he grew older, he campaigned for the wellbeing of the blind community and our right to a proper education. He also invented a more efficient system that allows blind people to read."

"How can someone read if they cannot see?"

"With raised lettering or bumps on a special piece of paper. Here, let me show you." Mr. Geoffrey hoisted himself out of his chair and sauntered over to the large bookshelf. She noticed his stride was measured, as if he were counting steps. When he reached his destination, he fingered the numerous leatherbound spines on a shelf at shoulder level. He eventually pulled out a thick, hardcover book.

"I acquired a few books from a gentleman who was acquainted with Mr. Braille," he said as he returned to the table. "Unfortunately, I have no way of interpreting this new form of lettering because he replied in French. I was hoping you could assist in decoding the raised bumps and then translate it into English. This could also be a good opportunity to teach me some French. It would help in my hobby of detecting unique dialects."

"I doubt I will be any help with decoding *Monsieur* Braille's book, but I am willing to try. As for the French lessons, I don't mind teaching you, as long as you don't ask me any more questions about my own dialect. Is that understood?"

"*Oui, mademoiselle.*"

She chuckled at his response. "Where would you like to start first?"

"How about a few basic words, and then we can begin decoding the book tomorrow?"

"*D'accord.*"

For the rest of the afternoon, Clair taught him a few everyday phrases to practice. She laughed at his harsh pronunciations and over-exaggerated nasal tones. He didn't seem to mind, though, because he smiled every time she laughed.

Clair was startled by her sudden cheerfulness. She had not experienced this much joy since her parents' passing. At first, this revelation unnerved her, but she ultimately chalked up her newfound glee to exhilaration from being charitable. She was encouraged by Mr. Geoffrey's change in demeanor in such a short time. He clearly benefited from having her as a friend, and maybe, she realized, she could benefit from their friendship, too. She knew she was treading in dangerous waters–to bond with someone she would only know for a little while–but she decided to set aside her fears and enjoy this novel, albeit temporary, companionship.

Chapter 7

Days later, Geoffrey woke to the stillness of the house. The waltz from his dream still reverberated in his head. He felt a burst of energy the moment he opened his eyes. He dressed himself in the clothes laid out for him the previous night before sitting on the edge of his bed to wait for Terrance to help him with the rest of his toilette. It felt like he was waiting for over an hour before wondering if he was up earlier than he thought. He peeked his head outside the room and heard muffled sounds of cleaning and sloshing water downstairs. He trekked through the servants' halls and stairways until reaching the swinging doors of the kitchen, where the sounds came more clearly. This close to the room, he also detected the familiar sound of Minnie's humming.

When he entered, she welcomed him with a cheery tone. "Good morning to you, young man! You're up early. Looking forward to another eventful day, I suppose." She tittered. "I do like that girl. She seems to be keeping your spirits up. You actually eat more of my food now. Speaking of which, I can make you some eggs and bacon this morning. How does that sound?"

"Thank you, that would be lovely. How early is it?"

"The birds just started a-chirp'n, so I would say six o'clock," Minnie answered over the continuous sound of a knife battering a wooden board. "Your friend will not be around for another three hours. Eat up, and by the time you finish, Terrance will be ready to help you with your shaving."

Terrance did, in fact, arrive right after Geoffrey took the last bite of his meal. They all took a moment to drink a cup of coffee–for Minnie, it was herbal tea–before heading upstairs to finish Geoffrey's morning routine.

After their tasks were complete, Terrance returned to the kitchen to enjoy his breakfast. With nothing better to do, Geoffrey walked downstairs and into the parlor. With the waltz still replaying in his head, he paced around the room, avoiding every obstacle with ease. He would often do this to improve his spatial awareness in the house. As he went about again, he miscalculated and tripped on the bench that belonged to his sister's pianoforte.

He struggled for a moment to regain his balance. Pain shot through his right shin. Frustrated, he plopped onto the offensive bench and rubbed his leg. Once the pain subsided, he opened the fallboard on the pianoforte and pressed a finger on one of the keys. The melodic sound was instantly soothing, and he played a few more keys. Soon, he was reciting a familiar melody, his senses lost to the music. He felt engulfed in a vibrant, solitary world of notes and chords, as if music swirled and danced around him.

"*Très bien, monsieur.*"

He fumbled on a note, which caused an awful discord.

"*Pardonnez-moi,*" Miss Clair continued, "I should have announced my presence."

"It's alright, Miss Clair. You are here early."

"It is five minutes past nine."

"I must have lost track of time," he said as he began to rise from the bench.

"Don't stop playing on my account. I rather enjoyed it. Was that a waltz?"

"Yes." He rubbed his neck in embarrassment.

"Who trained you on the pianoforte?"

"My mother used to play, and my sister would have me play duets with her when she was being trained."

"I did not know you had a sister."

"She is away at finishing school. She may come home for a visit soon. If she does, I will have to introduce you two. I think you will like her. She can be quite the troublemaker."

"It sounds like you two get along well."

"Yes, I hate to admit it, but I miss that little rat."

"I understand missing someone. My father could also play the piano."

"I did not know that."

"He didn't have many opportunities because there was only one piano in our village. He preferred the violin. He tried to teach me to play an instrument a few times, but I struggle with reading sheet music. I'm disappointed I did not try harder to learn before he died."

Miss Clair sighed heavily, followed by a long pause. Geoffrey longed to comfort her.

"You do not need sheet music to play an instrument," he said. "Here, let me show you." He patted an empty spot next to him on the bench.

"The bench is too small for us both."

"I will stand while you sit, then."

Once she was seated, he placed himself to the right of her. "Do you know the song 'Hot Cross Buns?'"

She giggled. "Every child has heard of that song."

"Good. I will show you what keys to play, and you follow along."

Staying next to her, Geoffrey searched for the right keys by counting the upper smaller ones. He played the three notes.

"Do you see how similar each set of keys are? Try to find a set for yourself."

Three flat notes rang one after another.

"Not quite. You are in the wrong key. Here, let me show you."

He leaned closer until their shoulders touched. He searched for her hand and, upon finding it, tried not to be distracted by her smooth skin and slender fingers. A strange sensation surged through his body. He turned his head in her direction, sensing her warmth, and her unique perfume filled his nose. The scent reminded him of cinnamon and springtime with its flowers blooming and sun warming the air. Then her shoulders shifted to angle toward him. Feeling her breath on his face, he had an undeniable urge to lean in until their lips touched. He was about to do just that when their moment was interrupted by the butler, Jeremiah, announcing, "A Miss Cunningham is here to see you, Mr. Geoffrey."

Geoffrey rushed to straighten his back and face the entrance. A woman's set of skirts rustled loudly as she passed the center of the room. He was immediately assaulted by an obnoxious perfume. This scent reminded him of acrid medicine with a hint of sickly-sweet flowers and lemons. Its citric odor pierced his nose to the point of sneezing before he was unexpectedly kissed on the cheek.

"Hello, fiancé. I see I am not the only visitor today."

"Miss Cunningham, what a-a pleasant surprise. You have met Miss Delacourt before. She is my, um, my tutor."

"Tutor?" she asked. "What do you need a tutor for? It's not like you are able to read sheet music, so how on earth could you learn to play the piano?"

His face contorted in frustration, but he wiped it away in hopes no one noticed.

"She is here to teach me French," he replied, "for our honeymoon to Paris."

"Paris?!" she blurted. "I already went to Paris last year. I had hoped to just visit family in New York after the wedding. No point in learning French anyway. Such a useless language. I guess we won't be needing your service after all, Miss. . . ."

"Delacourt," Miss Clair muttered.

"Miss Delacourt, you are free to leave."

A silence filled the room, broken only by Minnie, who must have entered at some point during this whole ordeal.

"I be needin' some help, anyway," she chimed in. "Come along, Miss Delacourt. You can join me in the kitchen. I will send along some tea to go with the refreshments for your lady friend, Mr. Geoffrey."

"I beg your pardon!" Miss Cunningham wailed. "I am not his 'lady friend.' I am his *fiancée*. I insist you leave at once, and on your way out, call for Mr. Jackson to join us. My chaperone went missing on the way in, and I would like to have someone here. I would not want our reputation tarnished right before the wedding."

"Miss Delacourt and I can stay if you like," replied Minnie. "While we wait, I can have someone search for your chaperone. . . ."

"No," interrupted Miss Cunningham rather quickly. "His father will do."

Without another word–though perhaps with a quick curtsy to Miss Cunningham–Minnie and Miss Clair left. An awkward silence remained in their wake.

Chapter 8

Clair retreated down the hallway behind Minnie, whose large hips swayed with each rushing stride. The moment they entered the kitchen, Minnie huffed.

"The nerve of her," she grumbled. "What is an unchaperoned, unmarried woman doing calling on a man? Engaged or not, it is unladylike for her to visit him. I swear, something fishy is going on with her." She took a second glance at Clair. "Why are you still standing, silly? Let's drink some tea and get to know each other. I'll boil the water. Have a seat, for goodness' sake. I ain't gonna bite."

Clair, still feeling uncertain about Minnie, stiffly sat on a large wooden bench in the middle of the kitchen. As Minnie put the kettle over the stove, Clair discreetly scratched her lower jaw.

"Is the face powder drying out your skin?" Minnie asked as she prepared the teacups, her back toward Clair.

"I-I. . . ." Clair stuttered.

"Don't worry," Minnie interjected. "It's not obvious to most folk, but I have seen girls like you try to cover themselves up with that arsenic powder, and it makes for an awful rash."

"*Pardonnez-moi, madame*, but I—"

"Don't call me none of that *madame* business. I prefer just Minnie. My friends and family have been calling me that ever since I was a baby. Looked just like a mini version of my mama, God rest her soul. I hope you come to see me as a good friend, Miss Clair. You look like you could use one."

Clair's lips trembled. She had felt intense yet bridled panic at the prospect of being discovered and denounced. In mere seconds, Minnie's comforting words assuaged those fears, and the sudden shift felt overwhelming. She could only stare at Minnie as tears threatened to escape.

Minnie, noticing her distress, rushed to her side and patted her shoulder.

"What's the matter, sweet child?"

Clair lowered her gaze, a trapped sob racking at her chest.

"So, you are not going to tell your *employeur* about me?" *she asked.*

Minnie lowered herself to Clair's eye level and took hold of both her hands.

"Oh, no, sweetheart, don't worry about me," she cooed as she stroked the top of Clair's head. "I ain't gonna tell no one. You can trust me to keep your secret. There is no judgment here. In fact, I admire your bravery. Not many girls can successfully conceal their identity as well as you."

The confessed admiration bolstered Clair's heart. Concealing her identity had left her isolated for so long. Minnie's words made her feel like she finally had the freedom to confide in someone. Despite being at Mr. Geoffrey's side so often, she still kept his newfound friendship at arm's length. She couldn't tell him her secrets. Until Minnie, she believed that no one aside from her parents would ever fully desire a friendship with her.

"Your words are *très réconfortante*," she managed to say, her voice trembling. "It has been a long time since I've experienced such kindness. I am so tired of hiding. I'm working so hard to find my new home out west."

"I understand, baby. Is there a place you have in mind?"

"I do not know the location. All I know is to look for a group of unusual people who will accept me for what I am."

"A group of unusual people?"

"My mother would call them uniquely beautiful, inside and out."

"Where is this group?"

"All she said was that the people may no longer be in the location where she left them, and that I am to look for a creek."

"Creek?" asked Minnie. "Like a stream?"

Clair shrugged. "She never clarified."

"Hmm. . . ." Minnie pondered, crossing her arms. "Your mama may have been talkin' about them Indians. They are pretty unique. . . . If she is talking about that kind of group, there's a tribe called the Creek that I heard about. Was your mother an Indian?"

Clair opened her mouth to respond but was interrupted by the whistle of the tea kettle. At the same time, Penny entered the kitchen.

"Good afternoon," the maid beamed at Clair the moment she noticed her. "Miss Delacourt! How's that dress fairin' after the party? Were you able to get rid of the stain?"

Clair quickly wiped her eyes and smiled at Penny. "Sadly, it was too far gone. I decided to reuse the material for other purposes."

"Sometimes that's the best thing to do. Minnie, is the tea ready for our guest?"

"It's steeping now." While Minnie poured the hot water into a fancy china kettle, she spoke French to Clair. "Once she leaves, I will prepare you a new kind of concealer. It will be gentler on your beautiful skin and not look like paint."

Clair nodded and waited patiently for the women to go about their business.

She inhaled deeply, feeling more at ease now that she had found a friend in Minnie. Her trepidations from this morning melted into hope as she thought about the personal leaps and successes she had already experienced today. She was glad she didn't submit to her desire to quit, and that her persistence landed her in a safe spot for now.

Clair sat back and enjoyed the camaraderie Penny and Minnie both shared as they helped one another prepare the serving tray, laughing about an incident in the kitchen yesterday.

Occasionally, Minnie would include Clair in their conversation, and Clair enjoyed being treated like an equal, for once.

"That girl," Penny sighed after another bout of laughter. "Something about her just doesn't seem right."

"What are you jabbering on about, Penny?" Minnie asked.

"Mr. Geoffrey's fiancée. She doesn't seem right for the boy. She's all fussy and he's . . . well . . . not. From what I hear from her travelin' maid, Miss Cunningham was practically kicked out of her family's house, but the maid couldn't tell me what for. Makes you wonder why her parents ain't here. The only one who'd be willing to chaperone her was her old spinster aunt who looks too frail to lift a feather, what with her always coughing and all. Then there's her randy brother who likes to grope the help and visit the brothels every other night. The maid thinks he was paid a large sum to accompany the ladies."

"Come on now. Let's not find ourselves lost in a swamp of gossip."

"I saw that girl's rudeness for myself just today. I was just coming back from the market when I saw Miss Cunnigham cuss the chaperone out before leaving the carriage by herself. She was madder than a wet hen. I knew she was talkin' to that poor creature 'cause as the carriage passed by, I could hear coughing in between the sobs. That girl doesn't seem like the upright Christian young Mr. Geoffrey ought to be marrying, if you ask me."

"Well, I'm sure there's a good reason for him to be gettin' hitched to the likes of her. You know how it is with these folks. They marry for money more than love."

"I guess you're right, Min. I'm glad I'm not rich enough to be in that kind of situation."

"Amen!" sang Minnie before chortling. "Ain't we all, right Miss Clair?"

Clair, immersed in their amusing conversation, was blindsided by the sudden inclusion. Her smile subsided as she thought about her aunt's arrangement with her cousin.

Noticing Clair's change in demeanor, Minnie added, "At the same time, folks in all kinds of situations have to marry someone they don't love. I guess we gotta do what we gotta do to survive."

"Ain't that the truth," Penny commented. "I'm just glad I found myself a man who loves me. He should be proposin' any day now."

"Bless your heart. You keep telling yourself that."

Penny wrinkled her nose at Minnie before turning her attention to Clair.

"How about you, Miss Clair. You got a man?"

A blush radiated across Clair's cheeks. "I'm finding my home out west first before I find a husband."

"I'll tell you what, from what I reckon, home is not a place but the people we love. You don't need to go west to find that."

"Amen, Penny," Minnie said. "I didn't always know where I was going to rest my head, but I knew I was home because of the love and devotion my husband and I shared. God rest his soul. . . ."

"It's a shame he couldn't see the life you made for yourself after the war, Minnie."

"Thank you, Penny, but God has a reason for all things good and bad. I am thankful we got the time that we had."

When the tea was ready, Penny grabbed the tray and used her hip to push open the swinging door. Before she left, she said, "It sure was nice seein' you again, Miss Clair."

"It was nice to see you, too," Clair replied.

Once Penny left, Minnie hustled about, looking for tins of ingredients. While she showed Clair how to mix the rice powder and other ingredients, Minnie continued her inquiries as if their prior conversation had never been interrupted.

"Do you have a way to get to the Creek?"

"I have been writing to a few companies that employ wagon trains, but many have not written back, and the ones that do will not allow single women to join."

"You need to find a group with a family. Them Mormon groups are a good choice, but I hear the men propose to just about any woman even if they already have three wives."

"Three wives?! That's blasphemous."

"That's what I hear. I'll tell you what, I may know a family a few towns away who has been thinking of travelin' by wagon train. I will inquire about it and see if they need an extra hand. They have a lot of youngins and could probably use the help."

"You are too kind. I would really appreciate it."

"No problem. You keep your chin up. I'm sure God has a way for you."

They talked a while longer as Minnie made the powder and explained how to apply it. Eventually, Clair looked at the clock on the counter.

"I should be heading home now. *Merci beaucoup.* You have been a benevolent friend, Minnie."

"We need to look out for one another. Keep your chin up, and hopefully we can chat again soon."

Clair gathered the powder–now wrapped in a linen strip–placed it in her reticule, and reluctantly left the warmth of the kitchen. When she neared the front entrance door, she was surprised to find Mr. Geoffrey standing there.

"*Excusez-moi, Monsieur* Jackson. Did I forget something in the room?" she asked.

"Miss Delacourt, is that you?" Mr. Geoffrey asked. "I was waiting for you so I could apologize. I am sorry for the interruption today."

Her attention was pulled to the parlor door as the butler carried out an empty tray. Inside, she spotted the elder Mr. Jackson sitting adjacent to Miss Cunningham, her hand on his leg."

"There is no need to apologize," she answered. "I am sure there is much planning to be done for your wedding."

He took a deep breath. "I suppose so, though I would prefer no planning at all."

Clair wondered if he meant he wished to just elope with his fiancée or if he didn't wish to marry her at all.

"Would it be alright if you stayed awhile longer?" he asked.

"Your aunt is expecting me soon."

"I won't detain you for long. I want to give you something."

"Alright. But only for a moment." Clair replied.

He led her down the hall to the morning room.

"I am sorry the room was such a mess before," he said as they entered the room. "I had not realized how neglectful I had been with the dusting. I mostly keep to myself, and I refused to let anyone, even the servants, enter this room for the past few months. When you had joined me that night, I noticed the room as if for the first time, and I have to say, I was embarrassed by all the grime."

"I hardly noticed," she inserted.

"Liar," he gave her a crooked smile. "With the help of the servants, I am in the process of cleaning this place. In my free time, though, I have been working on a project I like to call paper art."

He retrieved an object from a box on a nearby end table.

"I was inspired to make a token of our new arrangement," he said as he searched for her hand. The moment their skins touched, a tingling sensation crawled up her arm. He cradled her hand, palm facing up, and placed a flower in it. At first, she could not process seeing a life-like rose in the middle of winter. Its colors were vibrant with peach, yellow, and a hint of red. As she fingered the petals, she realized it was constructed of hardened satin. The stem was a wire wrapped in green tissue paper with leaves of green satin. Each foliage contained raised bumps to represent veins. She gasped.

"It is so beautiful and detailed," she said. "It's as if you have created a real flower. How were you able to arrange all the colors?"

He shrugged. "Penny helped me to organize them. I asked her what colors make the most beautiful rose. I told her red was not enough because your personality does not match just one hue, and you remind me of a spring day. She mentioned the color of sunshine in the morning. We then laid out the colors in order of construction–petals and leaves, then the stem's materials."

"*Merci beaucoup*, but I. . . ."

She let her words fall away as she shifted her weight. She dared not look at him, so instead, she surveyed the flower in her hand.

"Is something wrong with the gift, Miss Clair?"

"Oh, no! It is a wonderful gift."

"But?"

"I cannot accept it. I'm–I'm afraid you might be mistaking my friendliness as an invitation for a romantic relationship."

"It pains me that you perceive me as that kind of man."

"I do not wish to accuse you of being dishonorable, *monsieur*. I only wish to make it clear that I am not looking for a relationship that could potentially anchor me to one place before I find the home I am looking for."

"Miss Clair, that first night we met, and every moment after that, I grew to have the utmost respect for you. I do not wish to impede your plans in any way. This is just a gift to commemorate our friendship. That is all. And when you eventually depart on your journey, I hope you can take it with you as a reminder that you have a friend who is rooting for you and praying for your safe and successful journey."

Touched by his words, she held the gift to her chest.

"*Merci beaucoup* for your support. I will keep this gift close to me, always."

"*Je vous en prie.* You're welcome."

There was a moment of silence between them before he continued.

"Now, I must let you go. I wouldn't want to be the cause of my aunt's wrath. Will you return on Monday?"

"*Oi.* I look forward to our next session. Good day, *Monsieur* Geoffrey."

She kept the rose against her heart as she left the room. On her way home, she hummed a waltz and nearly skipped with each step.

Chapter 9

After the exuberance of the holidays wore off and Clair and Mr. Geoffrey continued to meet, the cold and gloomy winter days weighed on Clair, and she felt the effects of cabin fever. Although usually their exploits were accomplished in the dim morning room, Clair one day insisted they do their business in the brightly lit parlor room where the sun would occasionally peek through the curtains. She sat on a delicate couch next to the large window and surveyed the snow-covered landscape in wonderment. A light dusting continued to fall from a thin layer of clouds, illuminated by the sun. Clair imagined Heaven to be like the scene before her, except warmer.

Mr. Geoffrey sat in one of the thick, overstuffed chairs. They had just finished writing another letter.

"Miss Delacourt, I sense you are distracted by something," he said. "Might I ask what object is holding your attention?"

"Oh, I was only looking out the window," she said with a wistful sigh. "*De toute beauté.* It looks so majestic outside."

"Describe it to me, if you would be so kind."

"The snowfall is fresh, but the sun is out, making the white landscape sparkle like a million crystals. When the wind picks up, the loose snow blows off the roof and dances in a spiral to the ground." She sighed. "I grow tired of being inside where the only activity I can partake in involves sitting or pacing. The air is so stifling inside, and I long to be aroused by the brisk winter air. It would be a joy to stretch my legs and feel the way the snow crunches beneath my feet and see my footprints leave a trail."

He gave her his special smile that seemed only made for

her. "You have such an innocent way of seeing the world, Miss Clair. If you wish to go out for a stroll, by all means, do not let me keep you from enjoying this nice day."

Clair rose from the settee and skipped over to his chair. "Shall we go out for a stroll together, *Monsieur* Jackson?"

He scrunched up his nose. "I'm afraid my footing is not as steady when walking in the snow. The ice and uneven ground can be unpredictable and hard to walk on without stumbling."

Clair looked down, her shoulders drooping. "I understand."

Despite her desire to flee the confines of the house, she did not wish to leave her companion alone while she indulged in such a frivolous activity. She sighed, saddened by the prospect of being trapped indoors. She took a book from the desk and returned to the couch.

Geoffrey pursed his lips in contemplation. "Tell me, Miss Clair, is it a good day for an open sleigh ride?"

She perked up at the question. She had always longed to go for an open sleigh ride, but she never thought she would have an opportunity to do so.

"*Oui, monsieur!* I have already seen a few sleighs out on the freshly covered streets."

Mr. Geoffrey could not help but smile at Clair's enthusiasm. "Very well, then. Let's call on my father's driver. If he agrees that the conditions are proper for a ride, we will have him prepare the sleigh."

"Oh, that would be so lovely. But what about a chaperone? Minnie would probably not be able to join us. She is busy preparing the house for your brother's arrival."

"Many couples go on open sleigh rides unchaperoned. Besides, is a driver not a suitable chaperone?"

Clair did not know all of the American customs, but in France, it was usually an older woman who was the chaperone.

"Should we at least have Penny join us?" she asked.

"You can ask her, but I think I overheard her say she is feeling under the weather. Besides, when my brother was courting his wife, they would partake in one-horse open sleigh rides unchaperoned."

She put her hands on her hips. "We are not courting, *Monsieur* Geoffrey Jackson."

He let out a breathy laugh. "I did not mean to insinuate that *we* were courting, Miss Delacourt." He gave her a lopsided smile. "I only meant that if they are allowed to ride in a small sleigh unchaperoned before their engagement, then we could at least enjoy a nice open-aired sleigh ride with a chauffeur to act as our protector of propriety."

Clair rose and silently brushed the wrinkles off her skirt.

"I will get myself ready for our winter excursion, then."

She tried to contain her excitement, but her step was light as she all but skipped out the room. She felt as if this might be an adventure like the stories she used to read as a little girl–a sleigh, like a pirate ship, slicing through white waves. She had read of sleigh rides and witnessed couples soaring through the snowy fields in their sleek contraptions. Their wide grins and red cheeks from the cold and elation intrigued her, but she never had the opportunity to experience it. While she bundled herself into warm attire, a giddy flutter tickled her stomach.

Once everything was prepared, they walked cautiously to the sleigh. At one point, Mr. Geoffrey flailed his arms, his feet slid out in front of him, and he landed straight on his bottom. His face immediately turned red. Clair used every ounce of her strength to hold in her breath but to no avail. She hunched over as her bellowing laugh split the air. He focused his scowl on the source of the guffaw. When her mirth did not cease, his scowl twisted into a smile, and he laughed along with her.

Clair wiped away a straying tear. "Here," she said, "*permettez-moi de vous aider*. I will help you stand up." She extended her hand, and he searched for it. When their hands connected, even through their mittens, the touch made Clair's skin tingle. She used her own weight as a counterbalance to lever him up. Once he was hoisted to a standing position, he wobbled only a few inches in front of her. She gazed at his lowered face.

Their misty, frozen breaths intermingled. A shiver forming at the back of her neck descended along her spine. She felt as if his inoperative eyes were not only looking at her but also peering into her soul.

The idea made her uncomfortable because she feared what he might find. She cleared her throat and took a step back.

"The sleigh is only a few *mètre* down the walkway," Clair explained. "Would you like to take my hand to assist you the rest of the way?"

"Miss Clair, I would take your hand to the ends of the earth."

A blush creeped up Clair's already frozen cheeks.

"*Monsieur* Geoffrey, *tu m'énerves.* You are always so cheeky."

She gently nudged him with her mittened hand. The gesture must have distracted him because suddenly, his one foot skidded out of control. They were able to stay upright, but from that point on, Clair refrained from teasing and focused on preventing them from slipping. Mr. Geoffrey skidded a few more times, though, each one resulting in a humorous scowl across his face and a stifled laugh from Clair. When they finally arrived at the sleigh, Mr. Geoffrey did not enter it. Instead, he held onto its side and offered his free hand to assist her. Once they were both seated, however, he frowned.

"Miss Clair, where are you?" he asked.

"*Monsieur* Geoffrey, it is more proper to sit across from you."

He gave a little chortle. "I know you to be a woman of integrity and hold fast to proper etiquette, but the warming bricks and blankets work better if we share them."

She spoke softly, "*Monsieur*, I do not know all of your customs in America, but I would not wish to ruin your reputation if someone notices you and your tutor sitting so close together. They may perceive us as having an affair."

"I don't care what other people perceive with their own eyes. From my experience, it is often perceived inaccurately. The truth of the matter is I am going for a leisurely sleigh ride, like any other young person would on a day like today."

Giving in, she moved next to him and placed the blankets overtop their legs. Although she kept her distance, the open sleigh was considerably narrow. An electric energy filled what little space was between them. The driver, a brisk and burly man, glanced at the odd couple. He sniffed, spat on the ground, then sat on the driver's bench without saying a word. With a snap of his whip, the horses pulled on the harness, and the sleigh moved forward. Crisp wind grazed their cheeks. Clair heard the crunching of the horses' hooves on the packed snow and the whirring of the sleigh's runners gliding over the icy surface. A swell of joy lifted from her stomach and blossomed in her chest. Her eyes widened as they sped past snow-covered buildings. The solid, squared structures of houses soon rounded into white, rolling hills, snow-covered trees, and the occasional cottage or log home far into the distance. She imagined living in homes like that, out in the wilderness where the sound of nature filled one's ears rather than constant voices and wheels from the streets. She couldn't help but think back to her parents, who had always talked about living in the woods. An old hymn her mother used to sing crept into her thoughts and refused to leave. Her father would accompany the melody with his violin. Lost in memory, Clair began to hum along, unaware of the man listening beside her.

After a few moments, Mr. Geoffrey began to sing, "For the beauty of the earth. . . ."

Her eyes opened wide, and she snapped her head in his direction. "I-I was not aware I was humming aloud, *monsieur*."

"That is a very beautiful song. One of my favorites," he said. "Would it be too much to ask that we sing this hymn together?"

She squirmed in her seat. "I am not accustomed to singing a duet. I fear I don't hold a tune very well."

"Nonsense. You sing beautifully." Mr. Geoffrey took a deep breath before bellowing the first strains with a strong baritone.

At first Clair listened quietly, but soon the overwhelming sentiments of the song overflowed from his lips to her heart. Its pressure increased until her shyness was overcome by the desire to harmonize with the melody. The noises and scenery around them melted away, leaving behind their united voices.

After singing the final note, Clair's heart felt washed clean. For a moment, she forgot herself and settled closer to the gentleman sitting beside her. He lifted an arm and only paused a moment before placing it around her shoulders. They nestled close to protect themselves from the swift, cold air.

After a brief companionable silence, Mr. Geoffrey lifted his head to the chauffeur and shouted through the wind. "Excuse me, driver! How far are we from town?"

"We are quite a distance from town, sir! Be thinking about turning around soon! It looks like a blizzard is coming!"

Mr. Geoffrey returned his attention to Clair. "Tell me, what does the world look like right now?"

Clair meticulously surveyed her surroundings before speaking.

"The landscape is so beautiful out here. We are currently in a meadow. There are no houses in sight. It's so peaceful. The fallen snow is like a white blanket covering the entire view. The whole land looks pure, as if God came and erased all the blemishes off the Earth. I can see a creek peeking through like a snake slithering in the snow. The only colors are white and some brown from the trees in the distance. Even the evergreens are completely covered in snow. Although the sky in the distance is gray, the sky near us is bright from the sun shining through the clouds. This in return is reflecting and beaming against the white ground, making it so bright you can hardly see."

He nodded. "I had assumed it to be so bright. I can almost see shadows."

Clair focused on the blind gentleman. "*Pardonnez-moi, monsieur*, I don't understand what you mean. How can someone who is blind see light and shadows?"

He sighed and spoke patiently. "Many people who are

considered blind can still see objects but with limited detail. When I was younger, I could see lights and dark shapes. Now everything is mostly shadows, and my eyes briefly snatch small glimpses of light. Only when the sun burns bright in the summer or on very bright winter days does it appear in my vision."

Clair shook her head, stupefied by this revelation. "If you are able to see lights and shadows, are you able to see me?"

Mr. Geoffrey frowned, and his shoulders drooped. "I wish I could, but I am not able to differentiate objects."

"Many people believe you to be completely blind. Why do you keep this to yourself?"

He chortled and explained, "I am almost completely blind. I gain nothing by seeing a fog of light on rare days. For the most part, my days are full of darkness. As for keeping this secret to myself, I have kept nothing from my family. Their ignorance is their own doing. The world sees me as an invalid whether I am or not."

She tilted her head. "But . . . you are not an invalid. Whether you have sight or not, I have watched you perform daily tasks perfectly and independently, yet you allow other people to see you as useless. Does it benefit you to keep this from those who are close to you?"

He again chuckled and shook his head. "They do not care, and yes, their lack of concern has benefited me in the past. Before you were hired, people left me to my own devices when I acted the part of an invalid. Wouldn't you do the same to gain a better outcome for yourself?"

"Many people keep secrets, but it should only be used for survival. What benefit do you have to keep such a secret? You have all the resources to sustain you without the need to manipulate others. It makes me wonder if you have more secrets."

The air around them changed, and he tilted his face toward her and furrowed his brow. "Only one. . . ."

Suddenly, the driver shouted, "Whoa!" The horses

whinnied in distress, and the world became a whirl of snow and blankets as the sleigh slammed on its side.

Chapter 10

Geoffrey's world came crashing down in a matter of seconds. His whole body plunged and rolled into the harsh, icy void. As he lay face up, buried in the unforgiving snow, he felt an unrelenting urge to pass out. But the frozen encasement kept his senses peaked, preventing him from doing just that. He tenderly propped himself up with his elbows, ignoring the nausea churning in his stomach.

He frantically moved his hands around, looking for any clues as to where he might have landed from the crash. All he could feel was packed snow. The ground itself seemed to tilt downward. His upper torso remained higher than his legs, which meant he was on some sort of slope. Clair had said there were trees in the distance, but she did not mention anything about hills. This meant he must have landed on the edge of an elevated road or possibly the creek bed, and that he needed to navigate uphill. Any sudden movement could cause the snow to slide or make him tumble down the unknown grade.

His heart raced, and his pulse rang so loudly in his ears he could not think clearly. He breathed deeply through his nose and released it out slowly through his mouth, then repeated this process three more times. The fog in his mind diminished with every breath. The moment it cleared, the thought of Clair replaced everything else. The prospect of her being in possible danger put him on high alert. He tried to listen for anything that might give him an idea where the sleigh was located. The thick stillness of winter encompassed his ears. The only sound was the clomping of hooves in the snow and the jingling of bells fading into oblivion as the horses fled.

Just then, he detected a deep and masculine moan a few yards to his right. He focused, hoping he might hear any sign of Clair, but not encountering another sound, he moved toward the only one he could. With some effort, he rolled onto his belly. The movement triggered a shooting pain from his left ankle up to his thigh. Using his right knee and hands, he slowly crawled toward the moaning beacon. Geoffrey alternated his hands to check the space surrounding him, so as to not drag across any sharp objects. Inch by inch, he slowly trekked up the mound. Finally, he felt something smooth and solid. Occasionally, his mittens would snag on the surface, and he figured he was encountering splintered portions of the sleigh. He rose slowly and used the upturned contraption for support to stand. Once at the top, he felt something long and slightly curved floating several inches above the sleigh. The hard material was so cold that he could feel its freezing influence through his mitten. His heart quickened at the realization that he was holding the runner of the sleigh, now parallel to the sky. Before he could fully comprehend the magnitude of the upside-down conveyance, the voice became louder, indicating he was near the source. What started as moaning turned into cursing and cries of pain. Geoffrey gulped back a tight ball of panic in his throat and ventured closer. He was able to feel the driver's bench when the rough voice caught his attention again.

"Thank God!" a crass voice shouted. Geoffrey knelt close to the gentleman.

"Are you badly hurt?" he asked breathlessly.

The discourteous man shouted profanities. "Am I hurt?! Are you bloody blind?! Of course, I'm hurt!" The driver paused and then stuttered. "B-beg your pardon, sir. I meant nothing by it."

Geoffrey waved the apology away. "We have no time for apologies. Explain to me your condition."

The man hissed in pain and then replied, "Both my legs are stuck under the sleigh. They're twisted up somethin' fierce. I fear I may lose them."

Geoffrey spoke quickly, "I am going to try to lift this sleigh. As soon as I do, you think you can move your legs out of the way?"

The driver replied hesitantly, "I think so."

Geoffrey leaned back on the sleigh and used his one good leg and his back muscles to push. The cart lifted only a few inches, but that gave the driver a chance to pull himself free from the wreckage.

The man shouted in relief, "Thank the good Lord! Thank you, sir, for yer help."

Disregarding the man's gratitude, Geoffrey asked, "Have you seen Clair?"

The driver replied, "I can't see a thing. Only the sled. It's starting to snow perty thick."

Only then did Geoffrey feel moist, cold, thin flakes melt onto his cheeks. His body seized up from panic. It was the beginning of a blizzard, and he assumed there was no help in sight.

Without a word to the driver, he turned and moved along the sleigh. He kept one hand on the splintered contraption as a guide while he staggered through the merciless snow.

"Clair! Clair!" he bellowed.

With each shout, he became more and more afraid for her safety. After a few feet, his toe impacted something hard and thin. He bent down and picked it up, only to discover a long, jagged piece of the sleigh that measured from the ground to his chest. He tilted it to the ground and swung it from side to side as he slowly walked over the hard, cold snow.

He knew that as evening neared, the temperature would plummet, but adrenaline kept him from feeling the cold. The snowflakes felt more like thick feathers that lay heavily on his coat and skin.

He was losing hope of ever finding the young woman when his makeshift cane struck a soft lump that was different from the ice and snow around him. He quickly fell on his knees and crawled toward the unknown object. Suddenly, his hands landed on cloth. He hastily searched for any other indication that this might be Clair, but it all felt like a pile of blankets. Eventually, he encountered something solid attached to the pile. Upon inspection, he discovered a leather boot.

He whisked the mittens from his hands, which then scrambled up the lump of clothing, away from the boot. Soon, he felt loose strands of silky, curly hair. The whole time he searched for her face, the listless figure never moved or made a sound. Whether it was because of the cold or shock from the accident, Geoffrey did not want to believe that this limp person was his dear Clair Delacourt. He held his finger under her nostrils. He thought he felt the subtle sensation of air but knew that it could also be wishful thinking.

Tears threatened to well up in his eyes, and he trembled from head to toe.

'Am I too late?' he thought. 'Am I too late to save her? Am I too late to tell her my other secret, to explain how it was she who had opened my eyes and heart to love? That before I met her, I found no enjoyment in life? Through her eyes, I began to see a beautiful world full of awesome adventures. Even if I couldn't traverse the country by her side, my heart soared with the prospect of her fulfilled dreams.'

Now he feared his suggestion to go on this foolish trek may have kept her from doing just that. The anxiety of it all was too much for him to handle. He wrapped his arms around her and pulled her limp body into an awkward embrace.

"I'm sorry, my love," he said, her hair muffling his words. "This is all my fault."

He was nearly bursting with anguish when a small moan caught his attention. He put his ears closer to her mouth and waited what felt like an eternity for any indication that he hadn't hallucinated. He held his breath and waited.

Finally, long after his lungs began to demand air, a whimper escaped her lips.

With fresh tears streaming down his face, the young man threw his head to the sky and let out a breathy, "Thank you!"

So happy was he that he drew her closer to him. This time, she winced from the sudden movement. He gently cradled her.

"My head. . . ." she croaked in a faint voice.

She tried to touch her temple, but she was too weak to lift her arm more than a few inches. He felt around her loose, curly hair for any sign of a bump, finding one protruding from the back of her head. He worried that discovering her unconscious meant she may have injured her skull. He didn't know what to do about the head injury, but he knew that falling asleep in freezing temperatures could mean death.

He spoke tenderly to her. "Clair, my darling, please stay awake. Tell me, are you hurt anywhere else?"

She shook her head slightly but then it fell back.

"Clair? Clair?!"

He shook her, but there was no reaction. He scooped a handful of snow and planted it on her exposed clavicle. She gasped and her head shot up.

"I'm sorry, my love," Geoffrey said, "but you must stay awake until we find shelter."

She acknowledged his words only with a small moan. Now that Geoffrey knew Clair was safe in his arms, his mind began to process their predicament. He wondered if there was anything that could protect them from the cold.

"Driver!" he called. "Can you hear me, sir?! Are you still safe?"

"As safe as I'll ever be," the crass man said, unamused.

"Do you see any sign of shelter near you?"

"None, sir! I'm afraid the snowfall is too thick now, and I ain't seen a house for at least a mile or so. Even then, the ones I did happen to see were miles away."

Geoffrey felt all forms of hopelessness. He knew that only God could save them now. Maybe the overturned sleigh could provide some shelter from the heavy snowfall. He feared, though, that the sleigh would only slow the inevitable. No shabby form of shelter would keep them from falling prey to the harsh, deadly winter elements, yet he was hesitant to move.

Now that he had Clair in his arms, he was not willing to let her go, but he knew that he needed to do something in order to attempt survival.

He was just about to set the delicate woman down when he heard a subtle ringing of bells in the distance.

Chapter 11

Clair's eyes fluttered open. Dark shadows shrouded her vision with a warm glow of orange and red pulsating at a corner. She felt encompassed in a cocoon of downy blankets with the prickling sensation of a straw mattress beneath her. Her entire body felt stiff. She gingerly rotated her head toward the source of the glow to find the colors were intermingling in a blurry dance. From the same direction, she heard the familiar sound of sizzling and crackling firewood. She squinted to focus on what she perceived as the fireplace. Her vision, however, did not clear.

Clair rubbed her eyes. The sudden motion sent shockwaves of pain from her nape to her crown. The sensation brought back the memory of events before she lost consciousness. She remembered blinding snow and freezing conditions. She could remember being engulfed in someone's arms. She also remembered the faint ringing of bells before her mind dove into deep darkness.

Avoiding any sudden movements, she employed only her eyes to search for any familiarity within the darkness. The flickering firelight did little to accentuate the objects surrounding her. Anything beyond the light was hidden within the blackness of the night. She deferred to her hearing to sense anyone nearby, but only the howling wind predominated over the sound of the fireplace.

'Maybe someone is asleep,' she thought to herself, 'or someone may be hiding in the corner and waiting to attack.'

Clair's heart unwittingly began to race, and her breathing quickened. She flicked her eyes back and forth, hoping to find someone whom she may not have heard or seen.

Just then, a door across the room flung open with a sudden burst of radiance. Cold air rushed through the threshold, and a shadowy figure manifested inside the doorway. The large object appeared rotund and formless. Just as quickly as the door opened, it was shut again, and Clair was surrounded by darkness once more. The suddenness of it all startled her and caused her to jerk upright. This motion inflicted an enormous amount of pain, and she hissed and cried out in agony. A bundle of wood clattered as it fell to the floor.

The round figure stumbled toward her. "Clair? Is everything alright?"

She recognized the voice of Mr. Geoffrey. Not realizing she was holding her breath, she released a sigh of relief. He reached her bed in a few long strides and knelt next to her mattress.

Eschewing decorum, he left little room between them and reached for her hand. Clair longed for the comfort of touch to ease her pain. She allowed him to take hold of her hand. His skin was slightly cold from being outside, but the way his large palm encompassed her own made her feel safe. He rubbed his palms together to warm his hands before grazing his fingertips along her temple as he brushed away stray hairs from her forehead, then felt her skin with the back of his hand.

He sighed heavily. "Your fever has subsided."

He did not immediately remove his hand. Instead, he allowed his hand to slide from her temple and down her cheek until he gently cupped her face with his palm. His fingers were coarse but gentle as they caressed her skin. In a moment of weakness, she leaned into his touch. But with that action, an onslaught of pain assailed her injured scalp. She hissed.

Upon hearing her reaction, Mr. Geoffrey removed his hands and straightened himself. "Are you feeling pain?" he hastily asked. "Where does it hurt?"

"My head. . . ." she replied hoarsely, "and my entire body feels as if it had been run over by a horse."

"You are not far from the truth," he said as he put his hand atop hers. "The sleigh overturned. Do you have any recollection

98

of the event?"

"I remember us singing. . . ." she struggled to continue. "And then the rest is unclear. Where are we? How did we get here?"

He took a deep breath before speaking. "My dear, the sleigh overturned far from town, and there was no one in sight, save the injured driver. It started to snow heavily as soon as I found you. You were badly hurt, and I was worried you were. . . . I was worried we would be stuck in the blizzard. It is by the grace of God that a preacher was traveling home from his post office when he happened to spot us. He aided in your care and offered us shelter in his cabin."

"Where is the preacher now?" She looked around the room only to remember it was dark.

"He has gone into town with the driver to find a doctor," Mr. Geoffrey continued. "We discovered the driver's injuries were worsening. In order to save his legs, the preacher thought it best that he take the poor man to town to see a doctor as soon as the blizzard subsided."

"A preacher left us unsupervised?" she asked hesitantly.

Mr. Geoffrey chuckled. "It was necessary for you to stay here. You were unconscious, and it was too dangerous to transport you with a head injury and fever. I assure you, the preacher made me promise, as God as my witness, that I would not compromise your wellbeing." She could detect a smile in his words. "He even had me place my hand on the Bible. I explained to him that you were my tutor and that we had spent many times alone together without compromising anyone's reputation."

His words reminded her of their growing friendship and his trustworthy character. She relaxed into the pillow.

"How long have I been unconscious?"

"For a day and a half," he said. "The preacher left with the driver early yesterday morning when the blizzard subsided, but the winds picked up a few hours after he left. I fear another blizzard is passing through. He said he would return before nightfall, but it is now morning."

Clair furrowed her brows. "What do you mean by morning? How can you tell?"

"He has a small clock on the fireplace mantle," Mr. Geoffrey said. "It chimes the hour. It chimed eight times not too long ago."

"Are you sure you are not mistaken, and it is eight in the evening?" she asked, her words rushing forth and taking most of her air with them. She feared the true reason why the room was so dark during the day. Even with curtains drawn, she assumed there would be some distinction between the light and darkness, but there was none in her vision, just a perpetual dim blur. It unnerved her not to be able to see her surroundings, especially in such an unfamiliar place.

"I am sure. . . ." he spoke apprehensively. "I am careful to remember hours so as to prevent confusion between what is day and what is night."

She paused before speaking again, trying first to find reasoning before she panicked. "Are there windows in the cabin?"

"Yes. When I surveyed the cabin earlier, I felt glass pane windows with the curtains closed. Why do you ask?"

"It's very dark in here. . . ."

"I wouldn't know," he chuckled. When she didn't respond to his teasing, he became concerned. "Is everything ok? Are you afraid of the darkness? I can open the curtains."

She felt the bed shift as he rose and a moment later heard the rustling of curtains being moved. Her vision adjusted to a slightly lighter tone, but everything was still a blur, and she still could not differentiate objects.

Her breathing quickened, as if her lungs could not hold much air. Although all she could see was fog, she felt as if the room were spinning. She grasped for anything nearby to ease her discomfort, but all her hands could do was flutter about.

"Clair . . . what is the matter? You are acting frantically, as if you have seen a ghost."

"I cannot see at all. . . ." She mustered these last words before her throat closed up and her chest tightened.

"What do you mean you cannot see?" Mr. Geoffrey said, befuddled.

Tears forced their way out of Clair's eyes. She gasped in rapid succession and felt as if she were being strangled from the inside. She lurched over the edge of the bed, clawing at her chest.

"Clair, dear! What is the matter?" Mr. Geoffrey asked in alarm.

"I. . . ." she gasped, unable to form words. "Can't. . . ."

The bed itself felt as if it were spinning faster. She reached for Mr. Geoffrey and clutched his shirt collar. As she pulled herself toward him, her eyes rolled back, and she collapsed to the floor.

* * *

"Clair!" Geoffrey shouted as he felt her fall from his grasp. He threw himself to the ground after her. His hand trembled as he felt around her still form until he found her hair. She was face-down and unmoving. He gently turned her over and picked her up. Her limbs were completely limp. Slowly, he placed her back on the bed, gently cradling her head as he eased her onto the pillow. He checked for breathing and felt small puffs of air under her nose.

"Clair," he said firmly as he shook her shoulders. "Wake up!"

Her body resisted the shaking, and she moaned.

"Clair, are you alright?" he asked.

"Did I faint?"

"Yes, you must have been overcome from dehydration. There is broth on the fire. Let me get some for you."

He was about to get up, but she waved her arm, searching for him.

"Geoffrey, I think my head injury has taken my sight."

Geoffrey's chest tightened, and a scream raged inside his head, but he dared not let it out. 'Could an injury cause blindness?' he asked himself. He remembered a servant once telling him of a nephew who became blind due to a falling branch in a storm. Whether or not the fellow regained his sight, though, he could not recollect. He swallowed back the panic that lodged itself in his airway.

He forced a calm tone, but his words came out quickly. "I believe I have heard of that happening, but are you sure?"

"I can only see dark fog and a few spurts of light. It's as if I'm in a dark, smokey room, but you say it is morning with the curtains open."

He thought frantically for a possible reason for her inability to see other than blindness. He could not bear to think of her trapped in a perpetual place of nihility. Having to learn how to navigate every space around her without the help of her vision, to learn simple skills all over again. . . .

A small part of him shamefully found a glimmer of hope in this new turn of events. Without her vision, she would not be able to travel for a while, and she may have to stay with his aunt for a longer period of time. Maybe he would be the one to teach her how to live with her blindness.

He shook the thought away immediately and chastised himself for thinking such selfish thoughts. Geoffrey knew that Clair being cursed to a world of nothingness would be the worst thing to happen to her because she so passionately soaked in all the sights of the world.

He jumped up from his seat and stretched out his arm, hoping to find the window he had felt before.

"Are you sure the sun is not hiding behind the clouds? I can take you to the window to be certain, if you cannot tell from there."

As he felt for the wall, the door suddenly swung open. He paused and waited to hear footsteps or a voice to emerge, any indication that the preacher had returned. Briefly, he hoped that no one else had come to call on the man, only to discover two young people alone together. In the moments that ensued, during which the newcomer could be in silent shock from their discovery, Geoffrey began to rehearse possible explanations in his head.

Yet nothing but the whistling wind greeted them.

Geoffrey walked over and yelled through the driving snow, "Is anyone out there?!"

He received no response but for the wind wreaking havoc inside the small shelter. Curtains flapped and the fire sputtered. Blankets rustled from what Geoffrey assumed was Clair keeping herself warm. He called out one more time but still heard no response in return. He closed the door and placed the latch in its slot to keep it secure before returning his attention to Clair.

"What was that?" Clair asked, "Was someone at the door?"

"I was hoping the preacher had returned, but it must have been the wind that opened the door," he said. "I think his humble lodging is more of a shack than a one-room cabin. I felt around the inside of the building, and from what I could detect, the planks are rotting, and there are many exposed gaps between them. Hinges need to be replaced, and furniture needs to be repaired. I know preachers are supposed to live humble lives, but you would think his congregation would give him a more comfortable dwelling than this."

"Are you sure he was a minister?"

"The driver recognized him as the old pastor in the next town over. I hardly know anyone, even my own preacher, who prays as much as he does. He prayed the entire ride to his cabin, he prayed over you when you were unconscious, he said grace for our evening and breakfast meal, and he had us all bow our heads and pray before he left with the driver."

He went to the fire and carefully pulled a pot from the hook. Failing to locate a bowl, he filled a wooden mug with fresh broth and carried it to Clair, spilling nothing. He gave her a sheepish grin.

"Maybe you are just dehydrated and broth will help. I would feed this to you with a spoon, but I worry I may spill more than you would consume. Do you think you can drink this on your own?"

"Yes," she said. "*Merci.*"

He found her elbow and traced up to her arm in order to place the cup in her hand. "Be careful and drink it slowly," he said. "Take only small sips. You may not be able to keep this broth down, and I would hate for you to become severely sick."

She took a few sips while he remained standing beside her.

After a minute or two she replied, "I am finished for now," before placing the half-empty mug into his hand.

He set the cup on a table near the fireplace, then returned to his stool next to her bed.

"Have you truly lost your sight? Are you not even able to see the fireplace?"

"I can see a few blobs of orange and yellow light and shadow."

She rested her head against her pillow and moaned in despair. "*Dieu doit me détester.* Why else would the Lord curse me with this awful ailment? What will become of me if I do not regain my sight? It feels like a nightmare not being able to see my own two hands."

"It is something to get used to, or so I hear."

She was quick to reply, "*Monsieur,* I did not mean to offend you. I was not—"

"I understand." He held up his hand to stop her. In a surreal moment, he recognized how futile the gesture was and realized that this must be how she felt around him when she made similar motions early in their friendship. She couldn't see him, after all, and thankfully couldn't see his embarrassment. "I was very young when I became blind," he continued, placing a hand on her arm. "I do not remember much before that. I do understand, though. I feel for your predicament. If I could, I would sacrifice all my other senses just to bring back your sight. Hopefully that will be unnecessary, and you will recover soon. I am fairly sure I have heard of people regaining their sight from accidents such as these. If not, I know an excellent tutor who can teach you to live with your blindness."

"I doubt I will learn to be as graceful as you are if I have, in fact, lost my sight."

He redirected himself and sat on the edge of the bed. He tenderly held her hand once more.

"Do not fret. From what I understand, the Lord does not feel animosity toward his children. I am sure you will regain your sight soon."

"But if I do not heal, if I am permanently blind, how will I live? Forgive me, you have shown that blindness is not the end of life, but my passion is to see the world. I came all the way from France to witness the beauty my mother always boasted of in this country."

"I understand the trepidation you feel, but blindness should not keep you from witnessing beauty."

"What do you mean?"

"Being blind only enhances your other senses. Instead of seeing beauty, you hear it in morning birdsong, or you feel it in the cool, refreshing creek water as it flows through your fingers. I smell the beauty of flowers in the spring. I taste beauty in Minnie's cooking, especially her sweet chocolate chip cookies."

They both chuckled.

"I may not see your beauty," he continued solemnly, "but I hear it in your voice when you express your love for your departed parents and tell me stories about your little adventures as a child. The scent of your perfume is a beautiful mixture of all your experiences from France to America in one fragrance. My heart feels your beauty when you show kindness and care enough to listen intently to my words. I only wish I could understand your outward beauty all the more with my hands."

"I wouldn't say I boast any physical beauty."

"I struggle to believe that," he said as he tenderly cupped her face with his hand. "If you are willing, I would love to judge for myself."

* * *

Clair turned to the fireplace. The room was now a shroud of dark blue, but she could almost see the orange and yellow flames swaying in a blurred dance. As she stared at the warm glimmer of the fire, she contemplated his request. She was torn between her natural curiosity and her desire to guard her heart. She longed to know if he would still accept her despite her undesirable features.

The firewood sizzled and popped, and though the wind no longer howled with rage, there was still a low whistle as it blew against the old house. Clair faced the man before her. She could hear his even breathing while her own felt ragged from anticipation.

She placed a hand over his and nodded before letting go. He began by skimming his fingertips across her cheekbone. The sensation of his soft touch radiated tingles to the top of her head and made her tremble. He traced along her round chin and up to the outline of her mouth. She inhaled, causing her mouth to slightly open, which allowed him to drift across her full, open lips.

His attention lingered at the groove above her lip before tracing from the base of her wide, round nose to the bridge. She tensed, afraid of what he might conclude by her differently-shaped nose, but he showed no signs of noticing anything amiss. He continued to explore the rest of her face, starting from between her brows to above her forehead. Once he reached her temple, he found a curl and gently tugged it straight before letting it loose, then found it sprung back into its original form. "I have never felt hair like yours," he said. "It is soft like mine, but it curls like Minnie's."

She held her breath in fear of what he might say next.

He lifted her chin. "It only proves how uniquely beautiful you are."

Clair felt a sense of pride at his description of her. She thought back to her mother, speaking the same words about the people she once admired. It felt as if Clair was finally seen for more than just her flaws.

Her blush deepened while he traced the other side of her face. He let out a breathy chuckle, and she knew he could feel the extra heat he'd caused.

"So, you do blush, *ma belle Mademoiselle Delacourt*."

His finger returned to her jawline, then continued down her neck. She shivered from the sensation, her neck involuntarily scrunching away from his touch. "And now I know you are ticklish," he said with clear amusement.

When he reached the space between her clavicles, he stopped, ever so gently circling the dented space and causing her breathing to quicken. He leaned in closer, and she could feel the electricity in the air where his lips had to be mere inches from hers. His breath brushed her lips, and she dared not move. She'd never longed more to close such a small distance in her life–her body almost ached for it–but she couldn't bring herself to do it. If only he would. . . .

But he exhaled and leaned away. Cool air invaded where his warmth had been, leaving her feeling a new kind of bereft.

He cleared his throat. "Thank you for trusting me. Now I insist that I return the favor. It is only fair you see me, as well." He clasped and squeezed her hand. "May I?"

She finally exhaled. "Yes," she answered as he helped to place her hand on his jaw.

She was surprised to feel the roughness of stubble. His usual clean shave was coated with bristles, and the coarse texture tickled her fingers. She grazed his upper lip and emerging mustache, then traced the raised bridge of his nose and along his low eyebrows before circling his forehead. She mimicked the path he had taken with her but deviated when she reached his hairline. She slid her fingers through his thick hair, feeling every strand brush against her skin. He leaned into her touch and gave what sounded like a low rumble emanating from his throat before he suddenly sat upright and grasped her wrist. He cleared his throat and gently guided her to his cheekbone. There, she traced down to his jawline and neck, where she felt his Adam's apple bob as he swallowed. While keeping one hand on his throat, she placed the other on his chest. His heart beat strongly through his thin shirt.

He grasped her hand on his chest.

"Now you know my heart beats for you."

Clair quickly retracted but immediately regretted her action. She was glad she could not see the hurt that must surely be on his face.

"What is it my dear?" he asked tenderly. "What causes you to pull away from me?"

"I wish I could tell you," she answered quietly, "but I can't. It is not good for us to be this close to each other."

"Why? Is it because you are considered my inferior? I care not about your occupation or status; I consider you to be an equal."

She floundered with her words. She had no idea how to explain her struggles.

"There are many reasons. . . . I . . . I am not what I appear to be."

He sighed. "If you are talking about your outward appearance, I only saw beauty. Whatever the rest of the world sees, I do not care. If only you knew what I see on the inside, my darling adventurer. My beautiful bird. How spectacular and strong you are. Do not let other people keep you from flying to new heights. To new worlds. Although my heart aches knowing one day soon you will fly away, I will never regret the time we have shared. I thank God every day for our first encounter at the ball. You have shown me life when I no longer wished to experience it. I'm even grateful for the accident because it revealed how important you are to me. I will forever be grateful that I know you are alive on this Earth."

Tears formed in Clair's eyes. His words overwhelmed her, and it felt like the room was spinning. A sense of betrayal flashed through her. She thought they had an understanding. Any romantic attachment could potentially tether her to one place, caging his "beautiful bird."

"*Monsieur*, I see you as a friend, but we can have no further relationship than that. Please, speak of this no more. I am too tired, and it's too much for me to bear."

Before he could respond, however, bells jangled in the distance.

Chapter 12

A few days later, the Reverend could almost feel the silence in the sleigh that carried him, the young man, and young woman back to their hometown. He could only imagine how different the journey back home was compared to their initial outing. Where there was most likely chatting and merriment, as per usual on an open sleigh ride, there was now a weighty silence and considerable distance between the unhappy couple. The tension made the preacher uncomfortable, and he tried to keep the mood light as they traveled through the snow.

"I am sure you are anxious to arrive home," he said with feigned glee. There was no reply, so he continued. "The snow looks like it's already melting. I wouldn't be surprised if that was the last snowfall of the season. I can almost smell the spring coming."

The Reverend inhaled deeply to emphasize his point. He glanced at the girl for a response, and though she gave him a forced smile and nodded in reply, she said nothing.

"How is your vision faring today?"

"The light hurts my eyes, but I am able to see things more clearly now. *Merci* for your concern."

"I am glad. The doctor spoke of full recoveries from injuries such as yours."

She did not respond again and instead stared at the horizon. He assumed the young woman was deep in thought, and so he abandoned his attempt at conversation. Although he was not currently practicing his ministry, as a preacher, he felt compelled to help the troubled couple. He contemplated what he would say and prayed for God to give him the words. After a while, he felt God had not willed him to intervene, so he kept his mouth shut until they reached their destination.

When the city emerged over the hill, the preacher spoke over his shoulder. "We are almost to the main street now, young man. Where would you like me to go from here?"

Mr. Geoffrey's voice was hoarse as he spoke, "You may take Miss Delacourt to her lodgings in the center of town. Afterward, you may drop me off at my home where I will provide something for you to eat and compensation for your generosity."

The man chuckled. "Good sir, you don't have to compensate me for anything. I do the Lord's work, and sometimes that requires providing a temporary shelter for those in need."

"I insist you at least come inside for some warm refreshments," Geoffrey spoke tersely.

"Maybe something warm to drink would be nice," the Reverend conceded. It was not long before they arrived at a red brick house. As soon as they pulled up to the front of the building, an older gentleman exited the door and trudged through the slush. At the doorway, there stood a crass-looking, old woman. Both looked irritated and annoyed. "Where have you been?!" the woman uncouthly shouted to the passengers. "We were just about to send a search party for you! I see you have run away to elope! How dare you disgrace our family!"

The older man arrived at Mr. Geoffrey's side of the sleigh. His face was red, his brow furrowed, and he aimed his gaze sharply at the young man.

Anger seared through his voice. "What do you have to say for yourself, boy? I knew you were an imbecile, but I wasn't aware you were stupid enough to run away with the help."

Mr. Geoffrey sat as still as a statue. He faced straight ahead, his jaw clenched, and his lips tightly bound.

Miss Clair, her mouth agape, rapidly shifted her gaze between the older man and the younger.

"Excuse me, sir," the Reverend intervened, "this fine couple did nothing of the sort."

The older gentleman shot him a fiery look. "And who might you be?" he demanded.

"I'm Reverend Theodore Lloyd. I serve as a clergyman in a small town a few miles from here."

The man was not fazed by this reply. "Were you the one who performed the nuptials?"

Reverend Lloyd was taken aback from the question. From what he knew of his new acquaintances these past few days, they seemed to be an upstanding and modest sort. He was shocked that everyone assumed they would do such a dishonorable act.

"Goodness, no," he said. "I found a group of people stranded in the snow when their sleigh capsized. They stayed in my cabin while the blizzard blew by. This young girl is still healing from her injuries. She just recently regained most of her sight. She hit her head pretty bad and was unconscious for a few days. I did the best I could to care for her, but the driver was also in need of medical attention. I think it best that she sees a doctor as soon as possible."

Out of the corner of his eye, he noticed the old woman hold her hand to her chest.

"Oh, how dreadful!" she exclaimed. "Girl, come inside immediately, and I will call the doctor to attend to you right away." She glared at the young man. "Geoffrey! How could you allow this to happen? What compelled you to force poor Clair to accompany you on such a frivolous and dangerous sleigh ride?"

The Reverend stole a glimpse at the young gentleman who was still seated rigidly. The only time he flinched was when Miss Delacourt hissed and then mewled in pain as she exited the sleigh.

After she was taken inside, the elder Mr. Jackson pointed a finger at his son.

"I will deal with you later." He turned his attention to the Reverend. His frown shifted into a smooth grin, his voice dripping with honey. "I apologize for my impolite conduct. Children can get the better of you. I have not yet introduced myself. I am George Jackson. We are truly grateful for all that you have done, Reverend. Would you care to join us for dinner? You would be our honored guest."

He squinted in contemplation and squirmed in his seat. The sudden shift in temper unnerved Reverend Lloyd. Although the smile on Mr. George Jackson's face seemed genuine enough, there was a darkness in his eyes. An image of a snake appeared in the Reverend's mind. Like a snake, the older Mr. Jackson seemed to possess a shifty nature. This was in contrast to the younger Mr. Jackson, who always gave an impression of trustworthiness. Although the Reverend did not want to pass judgment on a man he had just met, he still felt a need for self-preservation.

"The days are still short, and I have a long trip ahead of me," he replied. "I ought to be heading back home soon."

"At least let me compensate you for your time and effort. Please drive over to my house so that I can retrieve my booklet."

The Reverend lifted his hand and was about to refuse when the wealthy gentleman stopped him.

"Let's call it a donation to your church, Reverend. You wouldn't refuse money to help your ministry, would you?"

The Reverend thought of his old church building—a windowpane or two boarded up, its siding rotting off, and the inoperable church bell with a large crack at the base. He didn't feel comfortable refusing such a contribution if it could help his former flock, even if that meant tying himself to such a dodgy man.

"If you insist, Mr. Jackson, on donating to my town's church, I will not refuse."

"Great! And while we are on the subject, I hope that, should you keep us in your prayers, our situation will remain in your prayers and no one else's. We wouldn't want to burden anyone with our problems. I'm sure you understand."

Reverend Lloyd swallowed a lump in his throat and gave a slight nod. "I understand."

After one more moment of intense eye contact, Mr. Jackson returned his focus to his son. "Come on, Geoffrey. I have a carriage waiting at the back of the house." He threw open the door and grasped Mr. Geoffrey's arm, ready to wrench him out of the carriage.

The Reverend quickly intervened. "If it's alright with you, sir, I would like to drive your son to his home. We grew rather close these past few days, and I wish to say goodbye to him properly. I will gladly follow behind your carriage."

The Reverend hoped the well-to-do gentleman would not dare ruin his reputation by arguing with a preacher. He was not surprised when Mr. George Jackson, with his lips tight and face red, silently nodded and stormed off. He probably wasn't used to being denied.

Once the man rounded the corner of the house, the Reverend turned to face Mr. Geoffrey.

"Young man, I may not know you well, but I have a knack for judging good character. From the few days we spent together, I can see you are a man of integrity. You pulled your weight these past few days by caring for the injured driver and Miss Delacourt." He was interrupted by Mr. Jackson's large and extravagant carriage as it pulled in front of the Reverend's small, rundown buckboard-turned-sleigh. After he snapped the reins to compel his horse to move, he continued speaking. "You have been respectful and diligent the whole time we have interacted. Why would your father assume the worst in you?"

For a moment, the Reverend thought Mr. Geoffrey would not speak, and so he was startled when the young man finally did.

"My father has not taken the time to get to know me. He often accuses me of being incapable of making rational decisions. I am engaged to a woman I do not wish to marry. They must have thought I had run away to elope with Cl–Miss Delacourt."

"Did you run away to elope? You can confide in me. I am not here to judge."

"It was an innocent sleigh ride. Miss Delacourt is new to the country and is not accustomed to our long, extremely cold winters. She seemed melancholy from cabin fever, and I wanted to lift her spirits, nothing more."

"I believe you. I remember taking my sweetheart on a sleigh ride once or twice while we were courting. Nothing like a brisk ride through the country to evoke joy." He paused for a moment with a distant look on his face, then cleared his throat. "Anyway, I am sorry to hear of you and your father's strained relationship."

The carriage before them halted, and the Reverend followed suit.

"I wish we had more time to talk," he continued. "I don't know how you communicate outside of your home, but I would like to relay my address. Remember this address and have a servant write it down for you. If you would like to talk further, have a servant send me a note, and I will return for a visit. After my wife and child passed away last year, I have taken a sabbatical from the ministry, and I have had a lot of time on my hands."

Mr. George Jackson exited his carriage and immediately trudged through the melting snow and into the mansion, not bothering to wait for the Reverend or Mr. Geoffrey to disembark. Soon afterward, a young man with brown skin dressed in footman attire appeared beside the sleigh. He silently handed the Reverend an envelope, then focused his attention on the blind man.

"Mr. Geoffrey," he said, "are you ready for me to escort you inside?"

Mr. Geoffrey stood. "Goodbye, Reverend Lloyd. Thank you for all your help."

He was about to step down from the sleigh, but the Reverend put a hand to his arm.

"A parting word, if you don't mind. I can tell you care deeply about that girl. It's none of my business, but as someone who understands how beneficial it is to have the right partner in life, well, let's just say, I will be praying God intervenes for you, if it be His will."

Mr. Geoffrey stepped off the sleigh. "Thank you,

Reverend. I will be sure to contact you once things settle down."

"Be sure you do," replied the Reverend. He snapped the reins, and as the sleigh moved forward, he said one last goodbye.

* * *

As soon as he entered the mansion, Geoffrey's ears were assailed by a keen, shrieking bawl. It was an unusual commotion that had not echoed in those walls for a long time. Intermingling with the baby's cry was a woman's shouts originating from the upper landing.

"Can someone please quiet that baby?! She hasn't stopped crying since we arrived. I am exhausted! Is there no servant available in this household who can take care of her?"

A familiar, younger masculine voice materialized at Geoffrey's side. "You have been tired since the day we married, my love!" Geoffrey, startled, side stepped away from the man.

The woman disregarded the man's response and continued ranting. "Useless wet nurse! How dare she become ill right before our travels!"

She continued her tirade but was ignored by both parties.

"Well, brother," the man beside Geoffrey said sarcastically, "the prodigal son returns. We've come all this way to have a quiet Easter holiday only for you to ruin it with an elopement."

Before Geoffrey could reply, however, his father stomped into the room.

"Geoffrey," he said sternly, "come to my office, immediately. Frank, help him find it."

Geoffrey's brother, George Franklin Jackson Jr., grabbed ahold of his arm and dragged him down a long hallway. Tired of playing the part of an invalid, Geoffrey tried to pull his arm away, but his brother's grip tightened. The pressure left his arm burning.

Once inside, Frank continued goading. "What were you thinking, running away with the help? To be honest, I didn't know you had it in you. I'm surprised you are showing your face so soon. I assumed you paid off the driver with the horses and rode off into the sunset. Where is your blushing bride? Already indisposed?"

Geoffrey's fists curled into a tight ball. He used all his willpower not to wallop his brother. He heard their father move to his desk chair and sit down.

"Now, that's enough, Frank. Apparently, your baby brother was just going for an extended joyride. Isn't that right, *son*?" His last words dripped with acid.

Geoffrey remained silent in his usual spot near the fireplace.

"You should be ashamed of yourself," his father reproached. "You embarrassed our entire family. It is improper for someone of our stature to go gallivanting–*alone*–with a lower-class, unmarried girl. Nevermind that she's a foreigner! What will people think? What about Miss Cunningham and your engagement to her?"

Geoffrey's nostrils flared. "It was an innocent sleigh ride. I was feeling cabin fever and did not want to go by myself. You allow me to be in a room alone with her every day as my tutor. Why should this be any different?"

A thundering clap reverberated in the room as his father slammed the desk with his hand. "You will not talk back to me, you useless boy! If word of your little rendezvous circles back to your fiancée, it will be the end of your engagement, and we cannot afford that."

"Father, why is this engagement so important? She clearly doesn't want to marry me any more than I want to marry her."

Mr. Jackson cleared his throat. "Her father and I are establishing a business arrangement. Your marriage to his daughter will bind it. It is imperative that you marry her."

"I refuse to marry that woman while my heart belongs to another. If it is so important, *Father*," Geoffrey said, his every word dripping with sarcasm, "then why don't *you* marry Miss Cunningham?"

The sound of rapid footsteps preceded a stinging blow to Geoffrey's face. The strike sent him stumbling into a nearby bookshelf. He braced himself against the wall with one hand while the other covered the pain. A faint "oof" came from the direction of his brother.

"That should teach you not to disrespect me!" his father bellowed. His hot breath and saliva spattered against Geoffrey's face with every syllable. "You have no right to refuse this union! You fully depend on me, and because of that, you will do exactly as I say without question!"

His father returned to his desk.

"You dimwit. You talk as if love has anything to do with marriage. Have you spent too much time sowing your oats with that heifer? I knew you'd grown too attached to that girl. You are an imbecile to think you could marry her."

"Because she is a servant? I hardly. . . ."

"Because her veins are tainted with Negro blood!"

"My little brother is a Negro-lover?" Frank chimed in. "Why did you let a darkie tutor him in the first place, Father?"

"Don't call her that!" Geoffrey bellowed. He had heard people use that deplorable word before about his friends, and he knew how insulting it was to them.

"What? Why? That's what she is, right?"

"She's passing as white, and that's what makes her deceptive. I am ashamed to say I was not aware of her condition until I had more time to observe her. She wore powder on her face, and her bone structure is similar to that of other Negros. I have also witnessed her spend too much free time with the Black servants. Only other Negros would want to loiter with their own kind."

Geoffrey, after rubbing his face one last time, took a deep breath and squared his shoulders. "It does not matter to me what is in her blood or on her skin. . . ."

His father interrupted him with a startling laugh.

"Then you are more backward than I had believed. It's unnatural to have relations with her kind, no matter how light her skin is. It's criminal that she has walked among us in disguise for this long. I have a mind to tell your aunt that she is harboring a half-breed. I can only hope she throws her out on the streets as soon as she is told the truth."

Geoffrey quickly took a step forward. "No, Father, please don't reveal her secret. Her arrangement with Aunt Glinda is almost finished. She will soon be gone and out of everyone's hair. I will do as you wish without protest."

"As long as you marry Miss Cunningham, graciously and without any more complications, I will not divulge Miss Delacourt's secret. But heed my warning, boy. You can be sure that if you rebel in any way, I will make sure everyone from here to California knows of her true identity. In doing so, the rest of her life she will struggle to find a decent job and a decent husband to support her, and all that will be on your head. Do we have an understanding?"

Geoffrey clenched his jaw and ringing, as if an inward scream, filled his ears as blood rushed to his head. He felt trapped. If he refused, he risked Clair's safety.

He had no other choice. He would risk his freedom for her own.

However, Geoffrey refused to cower and bow his head like a rebuked puppy the way he used to do when he was a little boy. He kept his head held high and squared himself with his father's location.

Through gritted teeth, he stated two words as clearly as he could, "Yes. Father."

"Now scamper back to your hole," his father demanded, "and do not let me see your face until your wedding day. Frank, remove him from this room. Once you are done with that, return so we can smoke a cigar and catch up. It has been a long time since we last conversed, my son."

"Certainly. I enjoy a nice cigar and brandy."

Geoffrey felt his brother's fingers begin to encircle his arm, but he jerked away and stormed out the room. He took long strides down the hallway, but Frank caught up easily.

"Little brother, in all my life, I have never seen you act this way. You are usually so quiet and aloof. Maybe it's best you keep hiding in your mother's old, dusty morning room until your wedding day. Father's face was so red. I thought he was going to kill you where you stood."

Geoffrey, keeping a hand on the wall, turned a corner and hoped his quick strides and lack of response would deter his brother from speaking further.

"You should be grateful, Geoffrey," Frank continued. "It is a lot of work to find a suitable woman who is willing to support you. Normally it's the man who supports the woman, but, well, you cannot possibly do that. Father may have been tempted to take the easy path and throw you in an institute instead."

Geoffrey spun around to face his brother. "Leave me alone, Frank. This does not concern you."

"Of course this concerns me, you ungrateful brat. Can't you see you are the source of everyone's problems? You wore mother to death. You stumble around, constantly needing someone to clean up your mess, and you almost ruined our family's reputation with your stupidity. You are nothing more than deadweight. You're useless and should be in an institute out of everyone's way. Or, better yet–dead."

"I guess now I know why you hate me."

"I guess you do."

"Do not fret, brother. I will be out of your hair soon enough." With that last remark, Geoffrey walked away and turned another corner, out of his brother's sight.

Every muscle in his body was tight, his head filled with pressure. His ears began to ring again from the stress. He was so distracted by his rage that he was not aware of his surroundings, and he collided into the side of a plump person.

"Child, what do you think you're doin'?!" Minnie exclaimed, exasperated. "You nearly knocked me and the baby over."

That's when he heard whimpering. "Is that Frank's baby?"

"Yes, this is little Lillian, and she is the cutest baby you are eva' gon' meet. Here, you should hold your niece."

Geoffrey waved his hands and opened his mouth to protest, but before he could say a word, she shoved the weighted bundle of fabric into his arms.

"Mind her head. She is only six months old and still very fragile. Poor baby. She just stopped crying not too long ago when I fed her some goat's milk. She must have been hungry for hours. From what I hear, her wet nurse quit right before they left home."

The slight heft of the bundle sunk into Geoffrey's arms and chest. The baby's warmth radiated through the thin blanket. The sensation comforted him, and he could suddenly breathe easier. He took in the scent of fresh clean clothes soaked in lavender, plus the fuzzy, milky yet clean smell that all babies must have that somehow made him want to hold her tighter to his chest. A sense of being home overcame him, as if this bundle had the power to calm his heart.

The baby wriggled, and her head, resting on the crook of his arm, shifted from side to side.

"Well, look at that. I think I see a smile. She must like you."

Just then, Geoffrey felt and heard rumbling and puttering from the baby's backside. A foul odor followed suit.

Minnie chuckled. "Or maybe that was just gas," she said. "I have her things in the morning room. The sunlight through those windows will do her a world of good. Let's take her there to change her diaper." She removed the baby from his arms. A sense of emptiness descended. His arms remained frozen in place, lifted as if he held an invisible baby.

"Are you coming?" Minnie asked. She sounded a few feet farther away than before. "I need to know what happened. I was so worried about you! Where have you been?" Geoffrey followed her voice as she continued to the morning room. "I'm glad you are home safely now. Is that dear girl alright? What happened? One minute I'm packing you a snack for your little sleigh ride, and the next minute everyone is in an uproar because you have not returned home. And then your brother arrived today right before you did."

Geoffrey waited until they entered the room before he expelled all his troubles onto her.

"I fell for her, Minnie. Clair was like a breath I didn't know was being withheld. Now that I have inhaled her air, I can't get enough of her. I thought I could ignore my desires. I knew I had to keep my feelings in check because I was engaged, and she did not want to stay, but then the sleigh overturned, and I thought I lost her forever. I tried to tell her how much I loved her, but she made it clear that she did not return my affection. I thought maybe to give her some space and speak to her again, but when I arrived home, my father told me I could not pursue a future with her because I am required to marry Miss Cunningham. If I do not, Clair's secret will be revealed."

"Oh, dear. . . . Maybe we should sit." After they found a couch, she continued, "So he knows about her peculiar roots? I was worried someone would find out eventually."

"You knew?"

"That she is passing as white, yes. She confided in me once she knew I was an ally."

"You say that you are Black; do you two share a similar likeness?"

"She has lighter skin than I do, her face is not as round, and her nose is not as wide, but her lips are fuller than most white girls'. She does a good job concealing most of her African lineage, but if they found out she has any Black blood, even a small percent, most white folk will treat her unfairly."

"I have a hard time comprehending people treating other individuals differently just because of their skin color."

"Is it so hard to believe? Folks treat you different just because your eyes don't work. You had a good mother with a kind heart and treated us people of color with respect. When she died, you spent most of your days hiding with the help, playing with our chilluns, and learning our ways with an open heart. You ain't never known our skin color, only our hearts, and you know more than most folks that we all come from the same Creator and deserve to be treated as such. But just because slavery ended, that don't mean people will suddenly have a change of heart. Most folk still see us former slaves as dumb Negroes because that's what they grew up believing. It will take many decades, if not generations, for white folks to learn we are people just like them, and we have a right to be treated equally. Your girl will have a hard time finding a group who will accept her as both. That is why she needs to move westward. I have heard stories where colored people are more accepted there."

"I just wish I could go with her."

"If you love her, let her go. It ain't true love without some sacrifices. That is what I had to do. I had family in Louisiana, but I had to let them go to move out here for my husband. Half my family and I was given our freedom when our master died. Had it in his will and everything. But my husband was not in our master's will and was sold to another plantation. I gave up everything to be as close to him as possible. His new master would not let me on his property. I worked as a cook in a free state not far from Tommy, hoping to save up enough money to buy his freedom, but then the Civil War happened. His master forced him to participate in the war as a gravedigger. He died before he could experience freedom. There was nothing left for me here, so I wanted to go back home, but my mistress died a few years back and left behind a poor, defenseless blind boy. I fell in love with that little one, and I stayed to make sure someone took care of him.

"I know you love Clair. You may not be able to go with her, but you can still love her through your sacrifice. Let her find where she belongs."

Geoffrey had no response to Minnie's story. His mind and emotions roiled from the new information about both women he cared for most in this world. The rest of the day, Minnie comforted and distracted Geoffrey by having him hold the baby while she attended to both their needs. All three remained in the isolated little room, unaware of the chaos that swept through the rest of the house.

Chapter 13

Late morning sunlight filled Clair's bedchamber with a cheery glow. She worked on finishing her sewing in a wooden chair under the window, which she kept ajar to allow a mildly cool breeze to freshen the stuffy room. She breathed in the sweet scent of damp earth from the melting snow as she focused on sewing the last of her new dresses. She intended to make only a few outfits, keeping them simple and practical for her upcoming move west. Soon she would be ready to pack and begin her journey. However, she struggled to feel joyful at the prospect of leaving.

She paused mid-stitch and dropped her project onto her lap. She looked out the window as she recollected what Mr. Geoffrey had said to her only a few days ago when he declared his love for her. In her mind, he knew that she was leaving, so he should not have confessed his feelings. She could never reciprocate them. She had told him before that she refused to attach herself to someone and thus keep herself from proceeding with her plan. And during the sleigh ride home, she came to the realization that despite leaving soon , she did still want to remain friends. She had hoped to explain this to him, but then a note arrived the evening of their return.

Dear Clair,

I hope that you are in good health. I hear you regained your full sight. Although I am so happy to hear of your recovery, my heart is heavy with the guilt of putting you in such a harrowing

experience. The ride home and the hours since has given me time to consider our situation. I regret to say, we can no longer associate with each other. I do not wish to be in the way of your dreams. For this reason, I will say my farewell to you now in this letter. I wish you safe travels and a prosperous future.
Soar with reckless abandon, darling explorer.

Love,

Geoffrey Jackson

P.S. Minnie, who is in this room while I dictate to my footman, also wishes to tell you she is happy to have found a friend in you and prays that you have a safe trip.

Clair was disappointed by this new development. She worried her lack of feelings discouraged him, compelling him to terminate their friendship. She would give him a few days and then respond to his letter. But how should she respond? Would she beg him to reconsider and remain friends? Would it be fair to him if she continued their friendship when he clearly cared more for her than she did for him? Was it better to cut all ties now before he was hurt even more when she inevitably left?

'If only he could come with me.'

Clair immediately pushed that thought aside. In all her planning, she never dreamed of sharing this journey with someone. Although it would be beneficial to have a traveling companion, she knew he would not suit. Not only would it be scandalous for a single woman to travel with a bachelor unchaperoned, but he was also unlikely able to handle the expedition. Geoffrey was capable of doing many things, if not everything he set his mind to, but his disability would slow them both down. She wondered how a man with no sight could survive such an unforgiving journey if the harsh lands out west required everything an average man possessed. Clair worried about her own capabilities after her injuries.

Madame Glinda expressed similar concerns once Clair was checked by a doctor. He explained that she did in fact experience severe head trauma. Her neck and a few ribs were also bruised but not broken, and her one knee was sprained from being flown from the sleigh. Her mistress asked Clair to stay for another year and heal from her injuries. This was followed, of course, by a lecture on Clair's poor judgment and her need to be supervised a little longer before being let out into society.

A small knock from the door startled Clair from her ruminations.

"*Entrer*," she replied.

A young chamber maid with strands of auburn hair escaping from her cap shyly popped her head into the room.

"Sorry to bother you, miss," she said sheepishly, "but Mistress Glinda wishes to see you as soon as possible."

Clair sighed and laid her sewing on the traveling trunk. She knew the quiet morning would not last forever. The haughty old woman was probably calling her to discuss more of the week's undertakings.

Clair delicately descended the stairs, taking her time to avoid agitating her bad knee. She walked into the morning room where she expected her mistress to be enjoying her tea but was shocked to find her awkwardly hunched over, clasping the back of her chair. The woman's already pale skin appeared whiter than snow. Her handkerchief covered her mouth and nose, then she clung to her chest and began to teeter. Clair ran to her side and gently led her to her seat.

"I will call for a doctor," she said.

"No," the mistress spoke frantically as she flailed her hand in Clair's direction. Clair leaned in closer to hear the words spoken between gasps. "I . . . have . . . just heard . . . some dreadful–no, *awful* news!"

"Madame," Clair intervened, "please take a deep breath and sip some tea before you faint."

The old woman inhaled one large breath and let it out through her nose. She then took a large gulp of tea. Clair hoped the tea was already cold by then or her mistress would soon have a new complaint of a burned mouth. Eventually, Madame Glinda proceeded to speak with a little more clarity.

"My nephew's house has been hit by the plague. His eldest son, daughter in-law, and infant grandbaby had just arrived for a visit. Most, if not everyone, has come down with fever and other unspeakable symptoms. I was not told much, but I fear some may have already passed on. . . ."

The old woman began to sob into her handkerchief. Clair felt the room start to spin. She could not sort through her thoughts in time. Only one thought stayed at the front of her mind: 'Is Geoffrey dead or sick?' Without a word, Clair rushed out the room and through the front entrance.

"Clair, where are you going?!" Madame Glinda demanded, but Clair ignored her distant squalling. She picked up her skirts and ran down the sidewalk toward the Jackson Mansion. Strands from her pinned-up braid came loose as she ran. Pedestrians who were strolling over the melted snow or riding in carriages looked on with curiosity, but Clair ignored them also.

She had not prayed in years, not since her parents' deaths, but she prayed now.

She begged God that somehow Geoffrey was not in his father's house. She prayed that he left shortly after his letter was sent. 'Maybe he was driven out of his home for being discovered alone with me.' Despite her fervent hopes, though, she knew she was grasping for straws.

The road to his house seemed to perpetually lengthen. What would normally take only ten minutes to walk felt like an eternity as she ran. Pain shot through her knee and all through her ribs, shoulders, and neck. Her joints felt stiff, causing each step to feel weighted as if she were running through a marsh. When she finally reached his large, gray, Victorian house, she struggled to catch her breath as she stood in front of the white picket fence that separated the yard from the gravel sidewalk. The large, bedeviled house seemed almost cheerful with the red shutters, grass instead of the snow, and birds hopping along and pecking for worms. A man donned in everyday wear materialized from the front door. For a moment, she almost thought Madame Glinda misunderstood the news, but then she noticed what he was carrying. His arms rigid at his sides, he gripped wicker poles that framed a stretcher behind him. Another man supported the other end and atop it, a white linen sheet covered a body-shaped mound. As they placed the stretcher into a wagon that read "Mortuary," she noticed a limp, dark blue hand dangling from beneath the white cloth.

The first man then grabbed a wooden plank and nailed it by a string to the door. The sign contained only one word in red ink: "Quarantine." Of all the plagues in her lifetime, only one took lives that quickly, and if it was cholera, then no one in that house would survive.

Clair could not maintain her strained composure any longer. She sank to the brick sidewalk. The outer layer of her thick, brown skirt began to soak in the grime and mud from the street. Pressure built in her head like a teapot filled with steam and no means of release. Her vision threatened to succumb to darkness. She grasped a white, wooden fence post tightly. Although the wood's harsh splinters pierced her skin, she dared not loosen her grip. The pain in her hands was the only thing keeping her from fainting. She could not thwart the tears from escaping her eyes as she looked toward the house.

More people stared at her odd appearance as they passed by. She could not hide now, not with her powder washing off from her tears and her hair spilling out for all the town to see. But she didn't care what people thought of her.

The men were about to jump into the carriage. Clair yelled out, "How many are still sick in the house?"

The rougher looking one of the two took a second to glare at her, then he snapped the reins to start the horse.

As they passed her, the other man called out, "We only retrieved the one deceased gentleman, miss, but we were told to be prepared for more. It's not looking good for anyone residing at the house. Best to go back home before the sickness catches you, too."

At that moment, Clair knew it was pointless staying

there. She reluctantly rose and started her trek back home, limping from overexerting her injuries. All she could think of was the man who may or may not be alive in that house. Many emotions overwhelmed her, the least of which being confusion, heartbreak, and fear. Just this morning she believed her feelings for him were platonic. If she harbored any affection toward him, it was that of friendship, or so she thought. At this moment, though, if he did die, she felt part of herself would die with him.

Chapter 14

Geoffrey awoke from a light sleep to the sound of sobbing. Through a lingering fog, he could not tell if the cry was from an infant or a woman. He rolled off the small couch and lumbered over to the basket that lay on the ottoman at the end of his makeshift bed. He gently placed his hands inside the woven container where he could feel the warm and still mound of blankets, its center moving up and down ever so slightly. His six-month-old niece was unaware of the turmoil outside of the bedroom. He went back and sat on the edge of his bed. Memories of the past few days flooded his mind.

His father was the first to show signs of illness. The elder Mr. Jackson refused to let the stomach cramps and extreme thirst keep him from spending time with his eldest son and daughter. They enjoyed an evening of celebration, completely unaware of Geoffrey and the child's absence.

Little Lillian was an agreeable baby who hardly ever fussed, even with no nurse to care for her and Minnie too busy to do it all herself. The night he arrived, Geoffrey spent most of his time holding the baby and dictating his letter to Clair.

The next morning, Geoffrey's father collapsed beside his office desk after skipping breakfast. Not long after the doctor arrived, Geoffrey's sister-in-law fell ill and fainted on the floor in the sunny sitting room. When they discovered that Geoffrey's brother, Frank, also had a fever, everyone was required to stay isolated in their own room. Geoffrey did not feel sick, and so the doctor insisted he and the baby stay in the morning room far away from the others while Minnie remained in the kitchen, boiling everything she could while ordering the servants on how to care for the sick. Geoffrey tried his best to do everything on his own to care for the infant. The first diaper change was disastrous, an experience he soon wished to forget. The second was more successful, and he quickly figured out a system. When it came time to feed the baby, he was given a handful of boiled bottles, rubber nipples, and a container of goat milk. He soon figured out how to place all the items in order to neatly pour and serve without too much time wasted. When he did need assistance, he would seek Minnie, who was usually in the nearby kitchen.

She personally left trays of food, milk, and supplies for Geoffrey and the baby, but she dared not enter their room. When needed, she would advise him on how to take care of the infant through the door.

When it came time to sleep, the baby only woke up twice in the night. Both times she would fuss for a moment followed by a brisk wail and fall right back to sleep. The interruptions, however, kept Geoffrey from being able to fall into a deep sleep.

He had no inclination of how early it was when he was awoken by this new cry. He sat half-awake on his bed, contemplating the cause of the weeping. His stomach churned with unease. Before he could interpret his inner turmoil, a knock on the door startled him. A distraught Minnie held back tears as she spoke from the other side of the door.

"Geoffrey, child, I have some grave news. Your father. . . . Your father will not make it past this morning. I'm so sorry." She paused, and her voice quaked as she spoke again. "I hate to add more, but the doctor thinks your brother and his wife are not long for this world, either. I fear you and that child may soon be orphans."

Geoffrey felt his stomach drop. He did not speak for fear he might vomit.

"I wish I could come in to comfort you," Minnie continued, "but the doctor agrees it is best we keep our distance until this is all over. He also suggested I send a letter to your aunt to inform her of your family's illness. I'm going to do so, and then I will come back with breakfast."

"Thank you, Minnie," he whispered, but he heard no reply save footsteps receding down the halfway.

* * *

Early in the morning, before the fog lifted, Clair woke with a dreadful headache. Her crying from the night before and lack of sleep caused her to move slowly as she performed her morning ablutions. She was still exhausted from dealing with the dreadful news only two days ago. She hardly slept. Every time she closed her eyes, she saw the dark blue, pendulous hand protruding from under the white cloth.

'I have seen death before,' she thought. 'I have seen my parents' lifeless bodies inside the caskets before they were sealed shut. The idea of seeing yet another person I love not breathing and being put in a box to forever be closed is unbearable.'

Clair blinked in disbelief when she realized she identified "love" with Geoffrey. She knew she had loved him like a friend, but this new kind of love felt different, like a devotion she had never experienced. Losing her parents was rough because of her bond with them, and though she missed them dearly, she soldiered on with the hope of fulfilling their dream. However, with Geoffrey, she felt as if she'd just found a mainsail for her boat, but losing him threatened to rip the canvas away and leave her adrift. With that sad thought, she descended the main stairs as the doorbell rang. Knowing that all the servants were busy attending to their distressed mistress, Clair took it upon herself to greet the unexpected visitor. When she opened the door, she was shocked to see a young girl no older than fifteen standing in front of her. She had long, wavy, dark brown hair that was pulled back into a fashionable hairstyle. She was pretty despite the tear-stained cheeks and flushed complexion, which she tried to hide behind a handkerchief. She looked up at Clair with dismay and confusion.

"Is this my Aunt Glinda's house?" the young girl inquired

133

hesitantly. "I don't recognize you as one of her servants."

Clair cleared her throat and introduced herself. "I am Clair Delacourt, Madame Glinda's traveling companion and currently her personal liaison."

The girl nodded. "I recollect a letter my aunt wrote speaking of her travels and her new companion." She extended her hand. "I am Annabelle Jackson, her grandniece. I received a letter yesterday notifying me of my family's misfortunes." Tears began to flood her eyes as she continued to speak. "I immediately returned home from finishing school only to find that the house is in quarantine."

The girl could barely speak the last few words through fresh sobs. She was nearly doubling over with grief. Clair swiftly moved to comfort the poor girl by wrapping an arm around her shoulder and guiding her into the house. She sat her down in the bright parlor room and noticed the servant girl with auburn hair.

"*Excusez-moi*, have the cook prepare a tray of tea and cookies for our guest, and notify Madame Glinda her grandniece has just arrived."

The servant nodded and fled. Not long after Miss Annabelle was settled, the old widow entered the room.

"Annabelle?" Madame Glinda exclaimed, "I did not expect you to arrive so soon!" Annabelle stood, and the two women exchanged a quick embrace.

"Aunt Glinda, is it true? Are they all sick?"

Madame Glinda proceeded to tell Miss Annabelle of their new woes. Clair was uncomfortable hearing the retelling of all the horrible events that took place inside that large, gray house. She tried to withhold the memory of the body being pulled into the mortuary's wagon but failed. She imagined Geoffrey's being carried on a flat board. Her lips trembled and her body ached from all the stress, but she held her composure, not wishing to reveal her feelings to the other distraught women.

Once Madame Glinda finished, every woman in the room sat downcast and troubled. No one made further comments. It felt as if they were all quietly waiting for the next shoe to drop. Then, after a few hours of biding the time in sorrowful silence, Annabelle declared she was tired and wanted to lie down for a nap. This left Clair and Madame Glinda alone in the parlor. Soon afterward, a servant came in with a letter and handed the small, folded parchment to the old woman. Her eyes rapidly swept side to side as she quickly read the note. She cupped her hand over her mouth, and the letter fell away to the floor, its movement reminding Clair of the letter she left at her parents' gravesite. She did not dare pick up that paper for fear of what she may see.

"Oh, my dear Lord in Heaven!" the old woman spoke in anguish. "Now my nephew is gone. Another soul lost to cholera. The doctor thinks there will be more casualties and is still barring us from the home for fear we may catch the illness. Oh, Clair, why must I have to endure more hardship? I had hoped my experience with loss would have ended with the Civil War and the deaths of my husband and unborn child. I didn't think I would live long enough to witness my nephews' passing, as well!"

Clair's eyes widened with the revelation of Madame Glinda's secret loss. The old woman was so distraught that she did not appear to have noticed her slip. Clair tried her best not to show her own despair. Which nephews was she referring to: the elder, the two younger, all, a mix? She'd heard that Mr. Geoffrey's brother and his family arrived the same day the Reverend had been kind enough to escort Mr. Geoffrey and herself back to town. Did they stay long enough to get sick, as well?

It took a few moments for Clair to notice Madame Glinda hunched over in her seat, her hands clasped on her lap and her shoulders shaking. When Clair finally realized what was happening, she rushed over and knelt at the weeping woman's side. She placed her hand over the wrinkly, spotted hands of her mistress. Madame Glinda did not react to her touch at first. She continued to cry, her whole frail-looking body shaking from anguish.

"*Notre Pere qui es aux cieux, que ton Nom soit sanctifié, que ton règne vienne. . . ."* Clair began quietly.

Eventually, long after Clair finished praying and her tears subsided, Madame Glinda acknowledged Clair's kindness by gently squeezing her fingers. They both stayed where they were for a long time as they mourned together.

Chapter 15

The next morning, Madame Glinda woke with determination. She had the cook prepare a hearty breakfast for all three ladies. During the meal, which was moved to the formal dining room, Madame Glinda spoke of her plans.

"Girls, I have decided I will not sit idly and wait until the dust has cleared. Considering my nephew's prominence in this town, I am planning a large funeral for him. There is much to do. I will need to hire a casket maker, an undertaker, and more servants. We will need as many hands as possible to prepare his house for a wake after the quarantine is lifted. I will also need your help with arranging the funeral wreaths and black crepe around the house."

Both girls glanced at each other. After a moment, Annabelle spoke first.

"Aunt Glinda? Will people be willing to participate in a wake at my father's home?"

The old woman flippantly waved her hand. "Of course, Annabelle," she said. "The house will be aired and cleaned from top to bottom, hence why we will need to hire more servants."

Clair nodded. "I am willing to help with whatever needs to be done for the funeral, *madame*."

Clair spent the rest of her day helping the widow and her grandniece prepare for the funeral. During the menial task of cutting black crepe and tying it to wreaths, Clair became further acquainted with Annabelle Jackson. She discovered the young lady to be amiable and witty. She bore a great resemblance to that of her older brother, Geoffrey. Although she did not seem to have the same mature and sensible nature as him, she was, however, smart and attentive. Annabelle would talk about her little trouble-making adventures and pranks she pulled in finishing school. Clair, in turn, spoke of her playtime adventures in France when she was young.

She and Annabelle got along well together, and their newfound acquaintance made the heartache of recent events a little more bearable. Although Clair still did not know the wellbeing of Mr. Geoffrey, they were informed after breakfast that the death toll now included the elder Mr. Jackson, his oldest son, and his daughter-in-law. Clair mourned in the darkness of her room that night. She not only feared losing Geoffrey, but her heart also ached for the young couple and their child, all of whom had been visiting at the time the sickness started. She wondered if that baby, now an orphan, was also fighting for her life.

It took a week to finish all the arrangements, and by that point the doctor took down the quarantine sign. Annabelle was anxious to return home as soon as possible to retrieve some of her belongings and check on those who remained there. Madame Glinda insisted that she and Clair join the young girl. Clair felt like her stomach wanted to fly out of her body during their slow carriage ride to the house. Unanswered questions littered her mind. She was so worried about what she might find once they arrived.

'Surely, I would have learned if *Monsieur* Geoffrey was sick by now, right?' she thought. 'Why would the sign be taken off the door if people were still unwell inside?'

As they neared their destination, Clair could see that the house still appeared chipper despite its interior's recent turmoil. Even the same old butler opened the door as soon as the carriage came to a halt. When they went through the entryway, Annabelle was quick to walk up the stairs. As she did so, Clair spoke to her mistress.

"Shall I retrieve the head housemaid, *madame*?"

Madame Glinda, needing the cane more and more these past few weeks, hobbled to the right of the foyer where the formal parlor room was located.

"I was going to have the butler do so," she answered, "but you may go if you'd like. I am going to sit here while I wait."

As Clair walked down the dim servants' hallway toward the kitchen, she spotted the last room at the end and recognized it as the place where she and Mr. Geoffrey had their first and only dance together, and where she received the flower gift from him. The door was slightly ajar, and she longed to peek inside. Finally, her curiosity got the best of her, and she opened the door a little more. She was surprised to find the room was still rid of dust and the furniture in use. There were glass bottles on the end tables and fresh linen folded neatly on the couch. In the center of the room, a basket lay abandoned on the floor. It was angled in such a way that she could not see its contents. She stepped in a little further, curious to see what it held. After a few small steps, something in the corner of the room caught her eye. Although he was faced away from her, his thick, brown, wavy hair was all she needed to recognize this person.

Before she could stop herself, she whispered audibly, "Geoffrey," and rushed toward him. Startled by her sudden appearance, he quickly turned around. Before he could say or do anything, Clair wrapped her arms around his shoulders.

"Clair?" he asked.

"*Oui.* I thought I was never going to see you again."

Once she spoke, Geoffrey immediately returned her embrace.

"Clair, my darling bird."

Chapter 16

Geoffrey's heart was beating so hard and so fast that he feared it would leap out of his chest. He stood there, stunned that he held his beloved. He used every sense to soak in her presence. He could smell her unique perfume. She felt smaller but not fragile in his arms. She sniffled against his ear, and he comforted her by stroking her hair and kissing the top of her head. He backed away only enough to cup her face with his hands before lovingly tugging a thin strand of hair loose at her temple. Almost automatically, she tucked it back into place while he pecked her forehead with another kiss and then gently tilted her face toward him.

As they leaned in closer to each other, a soft mewl emerged from the center of the room, causing them both to pause. Clair pivoted toward the direction of the small, high-pitched fussing that came from the basket. It was then that Geoffrey remembered they were not alone in the room.

Clair removed herself from his arms and walked toward the basket. She gasped in delight and inquired cheerfully, "Who might this precious little one be?"

Before he could answer, he heard rustling from the basket. He figured Clair had hoisted the rousing infant from her temporary bed. He frowned for only a minute, slightly disappointed by their interruption, but then smiled when he heard Clair coo at the baby.

"*Doux petit bébé.* You're a precious little thing, aren't you?"

He sauntered over and found himself standing right behind Clair. He placed a hand on her shoulder and noted that she did not withdraw from his closeness but instead leaned against him and rested her head on his chest. His heart beat a little faster, and he sighed in contentment.

"This is Lillian," he said softly. "She is . . . my brother's daughter."

He reached past Clair's shoulder and searched for the child's tiny hand. Her small, chubby fingers tightly held onto his. Clair giggled at the interaction, and he gave her his biggest smile. The happy couple stood there, soaking in the moment. Geoffrey's heart felt full, and his desire to kiss her was overwhelming. He angled himself to place her at his side and gently searched for her cheek, tilting her face toward him. She willingly craned her neck until their lips met.

The loving kiss only lasted a moment. The baby refused to be ignored for too long. She squirmed and wiggled as she cooed in Clair's arms. Clair and Geoffrey broke the kiss but remained close, their foreheads still touching as they chuckled in unison. Then he reluctantly concluded their embrace by stepping back, though they continued to pour their affections on the baby. For the first time in a long time, all felt right, and Geoffrey felt that sense of home again. He wished they could stay in this moment forever. But, just like that, his smile turned into a frown as the past few weeks intruded on his happy thoughts.

"*Quel est le problème?*" Clair asked, concerned. "Why do you look so *déprimé*? Is everything alright?"

He did not wish to ruin their reunion, but he had to share what weighed heavily on his mind. He placed his hands on her shoulders while she still held the baby.

He hesitated to speak.

"Clair. . . . My darling. . . . Before the plague ravaged this house, something was put in place that was out of my control. What I mean to say is: I still may be trapped in my father's schemes."

He sighed. He knew her silence meant she was confused.

"You see, my dear, after the accident, I tried to end my engagement to Miss Cunningham, but I was strong-armed into continuing our arrangement. I am still betrothed to another woman."

His heart fell to his stomach as his sweet Clair backed away. He could only imagine the hurt expression on her face, the thoughts she was thinking. He tried to explain further.

"My father used me as a bargaining chip for a business deal. Now that everything has changed, I don't know what will be expected of me. . . ." He wished to say more–how he would likely inherit the estate as the sole surviving male heir, how all his father's business matters would be his responsibility to fulfill, how the survival of the estate heavily relied on his soon-to-be father-in-law, how he had to consider Lillian and Annabelle's futures and securities because they would become his wards, and how he'd rather spend eternity in that room with Clair than deal with the real world–but Clair came closer and placed her hand gently on his chest.

"Geoffrey," she said affectionately, "right now, I rejoice in knowing that you are *vivant,* alive. I do not want to spoil this moment. For now, let us not speak of the future but enjoy what we can while we are together."

At that moment, footsteps echoed down the hallway. Soon, a familiar, friendly, feminine voice boomed in the quiet room.

"Goodness me! Clair, is that you?" cried Minnie. "I was about to tell Geoffrey that you was here, but I guess you beat me to it. I was just summoned by Jeremiah to assist Mrs. Jackson. I had heard you was accompanying Miss Annabelle and Mrs. Jackson. I am so glad you agreed to help the poor Jackson family before you leave town."

Those last two words pierced Geoffrey's heart like daggers. 'That's why she does not want to talk about the future,' he thought. He felt embarrassed that he forgot she was leaving. He would not blame her for departing. What life could he give her that she could not find better with another man, whether or not Geoffrey was engaged? Dread built in his throat with each passing thought. If she were to leave, he would lose her forever. Traveling with her was impossible not just because he would be a hindrance to her journey, but also, he was bound by his obligations to his family. Now that his father and brother were no longer here, he knew that he would be the man of the household, even if no one considered him responsible enough for the role.

Minnie continued to prattle as his thoughts weighed heavily on him.

"Geoffrey, did you hear that your sister is here? Thank the good Lord she is healthy. She wants to see you."

They all ventured into the sunny sitting room. It was a bittersweet reunion between siblings as they embraced each other with exchanges of tears and sorrowful condolences. They discussed plans for the funeral while Lilly was passed from person to person. She especially enjoyed the playful attention of her young aunt. The setting sun cast a warm glow in the room. Once they finalized funeral plans, everyone retreated to their respective[3] homes and retired for the night. They needed their rest, for they knew tomorrow would be a long day.

Chapter 17

It rained on the day of the funeral. It was not a dark and heavy rain, though–the kind one would imagine on a sad occasion such as this. Instead, gentle showers interspersed with a lingering mist that seemed to seep into everyone's bones. The sun tried its best to peek through light gray clouds; its rays reflected against the tiny raindrops. A chilling breeze caused people to tighten their black coats around them as they proceeded to the gravesite. Many prominent members of the community attended the funeral. Even the servants came to give their respects to their late employer.

The heartbroken parents of Geoffrey's sister-in-law were also in attendance. The elderly couple appeared so frail as they walked side-by-side. They held onto each other as they stumbled along the muddy path, with their canes, toward their daughter's grave. Grief twisted their faces, and they never made eye contact with the people around them but focused on the ground during the entire procession.

Once everyone arrived at the three eight-feet-deep holes, the preacher continued with the service. Many people audibly sniffled back tears. One young lady was crying unusually loud. Clair could not tell who the woman was because she wore a black veil over her face. Eventually, a gust of wind lifted the veil enough for Clair to recognize Miss Cunningham. No one had been able to find Geoffrey's fiancée since the day his father passed. Clair wondered why Miss Cunningham did not wish to walk with her fiancé and support him while he mourned.

The immediate family stood solemnly nearest to the gravesite with Geoffrey between his grandaunt and sister while

Clair remained behind them, holding the orphaned baby. The child was content as she looked around at the unusual sights. She was oblivious to the sadness that surrounded her. When she was not staring, she entertained herself by playing with a black scarf that was wrapped around Clair's neck. She squirmed and fussed only once when the funeral concluded with a final hymn. As soon as it was all over, the gravediggers lowered the caskets and began to shovel dirt into the holes. The rain picked up, but the sun still fought to be revealed. A rainbow appeared in the sky, but it seemed only Clair noticed it. Everyone quietly dispersed to the large gray mansion for a funeral luncheon and to rest and regain their strength.

The family members were the last to leave, and Clair followed a few paces behind them. Her heart ached seeing such a sad lot. She could only imagine the unknowns that weighed heavily on them. What would become of Lillian now that she was an orphan? Who would be next in line to inherit the estate?

Clair was busy the rest of the day, comforting her mistress and looking after the guests. She had no time to speak privately to Geoffrey about the letter she just received and the decision that had been weighing heavily on her mind.

A few days passed before she was able to see him again. She and Madame Glinda traveled back to the mansion where the lawyer planned to read the last will and testament. The wet, early morning brought a thick fog, and there was not much to see through the carriage's windows. She also didn't pay much attention to the old woman who sat across from her and so was startled when she began to speak.

"I fear much will change," Madame Glinda said as she gazed solemnly into the distance, "and I am too old to handle all of this new responsibility on my own. I have very few people I can trust to help me." She sighed and looked straight at Clair with determination in her eyes. "Now is as good a time as ever to speak with you, girl. Let us not beat around the bush about this. I know you are not of pure blood."

Clair's eyes widened and her mouth opened, ready to

defend herself, but Madame Glinda permitted no words to come out.

"I had my suspicions the moment I met you," she continued. "It was winter, and you still looked much darker than the white aristocrats around you. My suspicions were confirmed after my late nephew revealed to me your true identity right before he died."

Clair finally found the courage to speak. "Madame, I—"

"No need to defend yourself," the old woman interrupted. "I am not telling you this to condemn you. Although I am saddened by your lack of honesty with me, I understand your reasons for keeping your lineage to yourself.

"I believe you are all God's creation, and I hold no ill will toward your kind. I only say this because I am sure you would find it difficult and disadvantageous to move about freely if people discover who you truly are. If I can notice your condition, so can other people.

"I would like to propose a formal arrangement between us. Now that my nephew and eldest grandnephew have died, my useless remaining grandnephew will be next to inherit the estate and all its responsibilities. He is not fit to run this household, and I will find myself caring for this family all on my own. My grandniece is not fit to marry yet nor to live independently, and my grandnephew will need help even after he is married. I fear the lawyers may also force me to look after the orphaned babe. I will need assistance, and I know you to be a hardworking girl. It is a known fact that you people are just naturally hard workers–all the more reason to keep you.

"I entreat you to continue to work for me but now as my lady's maid. Obviously, I cannot keep you as my personal companion now that I know your true nature. I would not want to cause a scandal for my family if this was discovered. Besides, now that I know you are a halfbreed, I am aware I was asking too much of you to read and write as often as you did. I would mostly just ask you to aid in the everyday preparations and some light manual work. You showed great potential during the funeral planning.

"Either way, I will make sure you have a good, solid room among the other servants and a generous salary–far more generous than what anyone else would give you. I know how you don't wish to marry, and you will not be forced into any marriages. I would prefer it that way so that you can be available to me anytime I need you. This arrangement, of course, will only work as long as you remain useful to me as an employee. What say you?"

Clair sat stunned as she contemplated her mistress's proposal. Only then did she realize the carriage had come to a halt, yet she could not remember when the ride had concluded. As much as she pitied this unfortunate family and wanted to help, Madame Glinda's words struck an unsavory chord. Her words were meant to be kind but came across as demeaning. Her tone toward Clair had changed to that of a superior person pitying an insignificant individual. That kind of interaction was the reason Clair longed to move on and find the people her mother said would welcome her with open arms.

The old widow waited impatiently for her response. Finally, Clair made up her mind.

"I appreciate the generous offer, *madame*, but I made a promise to myself and my deceased parents that I would do anything I could to travel to the land they had always longed to see. Arrangements have been made, and I am set to depart next week. Please understand I hold you and your family in the highest regards. If it were not for my prior obligation, I would have accepted your offer."

Clair prayed that this was the right choice. She wondered why God would keep putting these distracting and confusing hurdles in her way. She had long-since decided that no obstacle would keep her from pursuing her dreams and cause her to break her promise to her late parents. She could only hope that her answer didn't burn any bridges with Madame Glinda, who regarded her shrewdly and almost looked on the verge of contradicting her.

However, the old woman merely sniffed indignantly and lifted her chin high. After another moment of contemplation, she nodded.

"Although I don't agree with your choice, I do respect your decision. I hope you have a safe and prosperous journey. As soon as the will is read, you may prepare to leave, and we will speak no more on this matter."

She then tapped the ceiling with her walking stick, and the coachman arrived to help her from the carriage. Clair could only sit and watch as the limping figure disappeared into the thick fog.

Clair lingered, still reeling from the shocking proposal. When she finally could control her breathing, she shook her head and walked into the house. Everyone–including the sister-in-law's parents–was waiting in the foyer. Geoffrey stood in the corner as far away as possible. He rocked the baby in his arms and seemed deep in thought. Clair lost her breath when she spotted him. She blushed when she remembered the small kiss they shared only a few days ago. She'd longed to pull him aside and explain her plans, but there was never a good time to do so. She didn't want to do it with numerous people in attendance, either.

Annabelle approached Geoffrey and willfully sprung the child from his arms. She then proceeded to playfully talk to Lillian as she sauntered away. As she passed Clair, she smiled and wriggled the baby's hand in a wave. She gleefully told Clair of all the baby's recent developments, speaking as if she'd forgotten that she had lost her last parent and oldest brother. It finally struck Clair that Annabelle, too, was an orphan. She'd been so preoccupied with the baby and Geoffrey that she'd all but forgotten the implications surrounding this young, cheerful girl. While everyone waited for the lawyer to arrive, Clair enjoyed the distraction of Annabelle's company as they both played with the small child.

When the lawyer arrived, he directed all the family members and house guests to enter the dark room that was once the late Mr. Jackson's office. Clair, who now held the baby, had no idea if she should join them. However, Madame Glinda gestured for her to follow.

"You can watch over the child and keep her quiet while the will is being read."

Clair didn't presume to sit with everyone, though. She and the baby lingered in the back corner behind Geoffrey, who'd chosen to remain standing alone. He casually stepped backward and grazed his hand against Clair's free one. Her heart skipped at his touch. Despite his grief and dismay, he still curled his lips slightly into a smile. After the brief exchange, he continued moving backward until he leaned against a large bookshelf.

Clair did not pay attention to much of the reading. She did not care for the legal jargon, and the baby was a welcoming distraction. However, while entertaining the baby with silly faces and a blue satin ribbon, an argument ensued that redirected Clair's attention.

"Are you to say," cried Madame Glinda, "that my blind grandnephew is to inherit everything? Will he not need a proxy or a handler?"

"W-Well, that all depends," stammered the lawyer. "What I mean to say is, if you wish to contest the will, it depends on whether the judge will find him fit. Let's move on, and then I can answer any further questions. Anything that belonged to George Franklin Jackson Jr. will be inherited by his eldest son when he becomes eighteen. However, because they only have one girl, she will inherit the money once she is married. It is to be held in trust until that time."

At that point, a discussion arose as to who would take care of the precious baby. Madame Glinda, of course, was the one who broached the topic.

The lawyer said a few more words that Clair could not understand, and then the frail, old father of Geoffrey's sister-in-law spoke.

"We are too old to be responsible for the infant," he said,

his voice just as unsteady as his body. "We do, however, have another daughter. She is married to a landowner in Texas. From her letters, it sounds as if her husband built a sturdy house to shelter a large family, and they are well provided for. She is raising four children and has another one on the way. I believe her to be the most fit person to care for our granddaughter."

"And why is she not with us today?" the lawyer asked. "Surely a telegram would have arrived with plenty of time to allow her to travel by train and stagecoach."

The aged mother cleared her throat. "We have been having a hard time reaching them," she said, her voice weak and wavering. "Their home is far from town and the nearest telegram, but we did send a letter and hope to receive a reply soon. Besides, she is so far along, it would be too risky for her to endure such an excursion."

"I see," the lawyer nodded, shuffling his papers awkwardly as the other women in the room began muttering to each other.

It was then that Geoffrey surprised everyone by speaking up.

"If I may be so bold, I will volunteer to care for my niece."

Chapter 18

Clothes rustled and furniture creaked as everyone in the room pivoted in Geoffrey's direction. The room was deathly silent. He stood as if ready for battle, his shoulders squared, his feet planted firmly on the ground and spread shoulder-length apart, and his fists tight. He knew this offer would come with push-back, and he was ready for their arguments.

His aunt, of course, was again the first to speak.

"Grandnephew!" she exclaimed. "How could you suggest such an absurd idea? You can hardly care for yourself let alone an infant. This is not an appropriate time for your silly antics." She sniffed in indignation.

Geoffrey stepped a little closer to his father's old desk to address everyone. "I am perfectly capable of taking care of myself and a child. I have spent most of my life training and gaining skills to be independent, and I do not require as much assistance as many people believe. I have also taken care of Lilly on my own, with little assistance, while we were under quarantine. I have grown fond of that precious baby girl, and I believe I can give her everything she needs and desires. I promise I will provide her a loving and prosperous upbringing."

The lawyer cleared his throat.

"Son, I am not refuting your opinion, but I am inclined to reveal the facts. You say that you can live independently, and I am not arguing if that were so. However, there is no solid proof of your ability to be independent. In the eyes of the public, and even your family, you appear to have been an invalid under your father's care. Furthermore, even if you could care for yourself, adding a child is too much of a responsibility. If I were to weigh the options, she has an opportunity to live with two able-bodied parents, grow up with siblings, and be cared for in a stable household. That is just considering the physical aspect of caring for the child. You have to consider the financial responsibility, as well."

"I, by law, have just inherited the entire estate," Geoffrey intervened.

"Yes," replied the lawyer who remained calm. "You have officially become a wealthy man, but I suspect someone may plan to contest this in court."

"My aunt, you mean," he retorted.

Aunt Glinda harrumphed. "I have a right to question your ability to be responsible with the inheritance. With your frail mentality, I need to consider your sister and her future. You may ruin it with your inability to make sound decisions."

"I have shown no reason for you to believe me incapable of caring for my family and our inheritance."

"I have seen your father care for you your entire life."

"You have ignored me all my life. These past few years, I have shown my independence by caring for myself without any assistance. I have nursed an injured person on my own. I have even cared for a baby while the rest of the household was sick. Let's not forget, I was also engaged to be married, for goodness sake! That must show some trust my father had in my abilities."

"And where is your fiancée now?" Aunt Glinda interrupted.

"I have not heard from her personally, but her parents wrote a letter stating she does not want to marry me anymore."

He wished he could see Clair's expression. Did she look relieved or shocked? Was she still even in the room?

His aunt began to speak but was interrupted by the lawyer.

"This conversation is getting out of hand," the man said. "I recommend you discuss this matter in private, and we can discuss the next steps concerning the inheritance another day. For now, we must think of what is best for the baby. This contest could take a long time, and this child needs a home now. I am sorry, Mr. Jackson, but I think it would be best if the child became the ward of her aunt and uncle in Texas."

Geoffrey's aunt boisterously agreed while a few other voices mumbled in accord.

"With that settled, we must decide how this child will be transported to her new home," the lawyer continued. "It will be a difficult task because it is so far away. Is anyone here fit to volunteer?"

"I certainly cannot take her," Aunt Glinda quickly retorted. "It is a far journey, and I am too old for such a trip."

The elderly grandfather spoke next with a wavering voice. "Our travels to this town for the funeral was hard enough. We have not been able to journey that far to visit our daughter and grandchildren before. I'm afraid we will not be successful if we are to go by ourselves."

Just then, a voice spoke up that rang true like a church bell but also quiet like a harp.

"I can act as her chauffeur."

Geoffrey shot his head in Clair's direction. His heart dropped into his stomach.

"And you are?" the lawyer asked.

"Clair Delacourt. I . . . was . . . Madame Jackson's traveling and personal companion."

"Miss Delacourt, you wish to transport this child?"

"The time has come for me to commence the rest of my journey," Clair continued, "and I could take her to her destination along the way. Around the same time that everyone fell ill, I had been corresponding with a family who is journeying by wagon train soon. We have recently finalized our agreement for me to join them. They already have a few children, and so I am sure they would not mind if I bring a baby with me. Their journey begins at a fort nearby to Fort Towson, Oklahoma, where we would part ways."

"Impossible! I have heard of terrible things happening on wagon trains," Aunt Glinda protested. "Hostile Indians and dangerous terrain. It is too dangerous for you and a baby to travel by wagon train alone, even if you are with another family. I will pay all the expenses required for you and the baby to travel by locomotive and then stagecoach the rest of the way. I am sure you are capable of the journey, but I will accept no protest; this is for the child's benefit. Once she is safely transported to her new home, you can choose to travel however and wherever you wish."

"It is practically unheard of for a single woman to travel alone," the lawyer added.

"We don't have much time to find an alternative solution," Aunt Glinda replied. "I will hire a servant to escort her."

"Miss Delacourt, are you sure you want to take on this responsibility?" the lawyer asked.
In the brief pause that followed, Geoffrey found he couldn't breathe.

Her voice spoke with a definitive, "I am."

"Then it is settled," replied the lawyer.

Geoffrey, shocked by the exchange, could barely muster a word. "Clair...."

His voice shook in uncertainty. His heart felt heavy, as if Clair herself were reaching inside his chest and crushing his heart with her own hand.

"*Je suis vraiment désolé*. This is the best way to help everyone." Her beautiful voice rang with a clarity tinged with sadness.

Geoffrey's head spun. Unable to process this new development, he stormed out of the room, speechless. His emotions soared and plummeted as he ruminated on all that was happening. Lillian, the one he grew to love, was being taken away from him, as if he wasn't allowed to have even that small source of love. He had hoped he could be more or less a father to her. But to make matters worse, he would also soon lose his precious bird, this beautiful woman he loved more than anything else in the world. He knew she would leave him for a better life–she had a promising future full of adventure, happiness, and love–but for a moment, when the three of them had stood nestled like a family, he had hoped she'd decided to stay. Instead, he would be stuck here forever, left behind with a broken heart.

Chapter 19

The commotion after Geoffrey's volunteering and subsequent disappointment caused Lillian to become uncomfortable, and she squirmed and fussed in Clair's arms. People were now talking about travel plans, but Clair could not concentrate on what anyone was saying. She took this opportunity to escape the stuffy, dark room. The abandoned parlor room contained some of the child's belongings, and Clair hoped to find something to comfort her.

The moment she walked into the room, however, she spotted Geoffrey at the other end, bracing himself against the wall with his forearm. At first, he was as still as a leaning statue, and then he used his free fist to pound the wallpaper-covered wood. This startled the baby, and she began to cry. He turned suddenly toward the source of the noise. With long strides, he rushed to the sobbing child. Immediately, she reached her tiny arms out to him. He took her gently from Clair's arms and bounced her for a few moments, murmuring soothing words of apology before cradling her. Gradually, the child's fears abated and her tears quieted. Without a word, Clair watched as he lulled the baby to sleep with a soft lullaby. Again, she was amazed at his melodic voice and vigilance toward the baby. She wanted to comfort him just as he was comforting his niece. She placed her hand gently on his forearm, and he freed one hand to place over hers.

After another few moments, Clair whispered, "I think she is finally asleep."

She found an empty dresser drawer and placed her shawl inside, then she gently took the baby from Geoffrey and placed her into the makeshift cradle. The child stirred once but continued to sleep soundly.

Clair, seeing Geoffrey's downcast face and tears forming in his eyes, turned and placed herself in front of him, pressing close. She put one hand on his chest and used the other to caress his jaw. He leaned into her palm and placed his hand overtop hers. After a moment, she laid her head on his chest, and he embraced her. He kissed the top of her head, and Clair refused to look up for fear they may kiss. She knew that one act would make her change everything and stay with him.

After a long time of holding each other, Clair finally let go. She returned to the makeshift cradle and gently picked up the sleeping baby girl.

She kept her gaze on Lillian as she whispered, "The lawyer and your family are in the process of making arrangements for me to transport the baby to her new home. The sooner we take her to the ranch, the better it is for her to acclimate to her new life."

He took a deep, ragged breath and solemnly nodded. He didn't move from his spot in the center of the room. She headed for the door but paused when she passed him. While holding the baby, she lightly placed her hand on his upper arm.

"I will never forget you, my precious bird," he whispered.

"Nor will I forget you, *monsieur*," Clair replied, her voice quivering from withheld tears.

And just like that, she removed her delicate hand from his arm and walked out the room without another word.

Chapter 20

Days passed, but Geoffrey could not discern how long it had been since the heartbreaking farewell. After Clair left him standing in the middle of the parlor room, he fled to the morning room. The sun rose and set many times, but Geoffrey could not tell whether it was day or night. The heavy curtains were drawn closed and remained closed, preventing the sun's heat from entering and muffling the mild twittering of birds. The only way he could determine the hour of day was when Penny entered the room each mealtime to insist that he eat. Minnie was not home. She had agreed to escort Clair to Oklahoma. The two women would travel together with Lilian as far as Louisiana; Minnie had expressed her desire to visit family who lived down there. This was yet another blow that Goeffrey had to process because she did not say when she would return, or if.

Although his sister was concerned and asked after his wellbeing, she and the rest of his family mostly left him alone. He spent his days pacing around the room, restlessly sleeping on his mother's old sofa or lying flat on his back in the middle of the floor. All the while, he was contemplating all that had happened during these past few months. He mourned the loss of his family members. He lamented over the short time he'd had with his precious niece. Most often, though, he thought about Clair and the time they'd spent together. He envisioned the life they could have shared, and he grieved over the fact that they would never be together.

After what felt like a lifetime, Penny poked her head in to tell Geoffrey that he had a visitor. He was lying on his back on the floor with his knees bent and his hands covering his face. The footsteps sounding from down the hall reminded him of his father's distinct tapping of bootheels against the floor. But as the stranger entered the room, Geoffrey was too drained and too tired to say anything.

"I guess I'll leave you two alone," Penny said. "I'll be just down the hallway in the kitchen. Holler if you need anything," she added as she closed the door.

For the longest time, Geoffrey stayed unmoving. The stranger sat on one of the old chairs against the wall. Eventually, he broke the silence with a familiar and calm voice.

"It seems much has happened since we last met, young lad." He paused for a moment, as if lost for words. "I was praying that God would give me a chance to see how you fared after we parted ways at the end of winter," he continued cautiously. "It was not long ago that I heard about your family's passing. I am sorry about your father, brother, and sister-in-law. I hear this plague is unforgiving as it ravages from town to town."

Geoffrey rose to a seated position and turned his head contemplatively toward the gentleman. He must have looked confused in his incredulity.

The man chuckled. "I guess you wouldn't recognize me from just the sound of my voice. I am—"

"Reverend Lloyd," Geoffrey finished for him. His throat hurt from the dry air and lack of speaking. "I remember you now."

"I am glad that you remember. How mindful and intelligent you are. You showed me a lot of your abilities when you and your young lady friend were stuck in that predicament. Speaking of which, I was surprised to hear she is about to embark on a long journey. They told me she is to take your orphaned niece to her aunt and uncle's home. When I heard she was catching the first train out of my town tomorrow, I was going to offer Miss Delacourt a ride myself, but they said she had already left. I guess she needed to shop around town for supplies before she boarded the train. It is no easy feat to travel with a baby. She is a good woman for offering her services like that."

Geoffrey's face became even more downcast when he heard Clair's name and her pending departure. He had held a glimmer of hope that she might change her mind and stay, but now she was near the point of no return. He covered his face with his hands and moaned with grief.

"What seems to be the problem, son? You look so forlorn. Is it the loss of your family or the loss of your lady friend?"

Although surprised by the Reverend's bold inquiry, Geoffrey felt he could be honest with this man of God. His frank but open and accepting nature made him one of the few people around which Geoffrey felt comfortable being himself. He lowered his hands.

"Reverend, I am saddened by the loss of my family, but it is a grief I have felt before. I am feeling a new kind now; I am bereft. It is as if part of me has been taken away. She made me whole, and now I am broken in two. I love her so much, and I know she would not be happy if she chose to stay here. She needs to do what she set out to accomplish, but I only wish she would let me accompany her. I know that sounds preposterous."

The older man sighed. "Why is it so far-fetched that you cannot travel with her?"

Geoffrey gestured at himself. "Look at me. I am useless. I will only be a burden and not the husband she deserves. Everyone believes it, now so must I."

"Where you are weak, God is strong. Do you have faith He will provide for you?"

"With all due respect, Reverend, I have not relied on God for a long time."

"You may not have directly asked Him for anything, but He has had a hand in your entire life. He has provided for you in so many ways."

"Then it is safe to say God is the cause of my troubles."

The Reverend crouched beside Geoffrey and placed a broad comforting hand on his back.

"Yes. That is true. He allowed you to be blind, but that

does not mean it was for naught. All that He allows in this world, if you trust in Him, is for good. My family dying was unbearable, and I was angry with God. I did not understand why He would allow them to die, but after a while, I saw the good in His plan. Their passing brought me to a place where I was able to prevent a group of people from perishing in the cold.

"I am not saying I understand what good your blindness brings, but if you have faith–faith as small as a mustard seed– then you will see for yourself one day the purpose of your complicated and wonderful life.

"From what I have witnessed this winter surrounding the accident, I believe you to be an independent and capable man. I have no doubt you are competent enough to care for yourself while also caring for others. The journey ahead may be harder for you than other folks, but I know you are capable of many things. I believe, with God's help, you can be a strong and supportive husband for Miss Delacourt. If it is God's will, He is going to use your partnership to accomplish great things."

A new hope arose in Geoffrey's heart. He asked hesitantly, "How do I know if it is God's will?"

"Pray for wisdom, and then be sure to take whatever leaps He commands you to take," replied the Reverend.

"Leaping is not easy for a blind man," Geoffrey responded.

The preacher chuckled. "It's not easy for a man with sight, either. Even I, a man of the cloth, find it hard to leap at times."

Geoffrey decided at that moment to bow his head and silently pray for guidance. The Reverend took his cue and prayed silently alongside him. After spending time quietly thanking, requesting, and listening to God, Geoffrey felt a comforting peace flow through him. It mixed with exhilaration as he raised his head and declared, "I know what I need to do."

Chapter 21

Clair paced around her small boarding house room. It was cozy and clean, but it was not as peaceful and quiet as she had hoped. The other tenants could be heard chattering beneath her floor where the dining hall was located. Still, her heart raced with the excitement of her journey finally continuing. Minnie had just finished packing the remaining items they had purchased earlier that day, including a wicker traveling bassinet. A carpet bag held a few spare bottles and an extra set of clothes for the baby.

"I'm afraid I don't have any more room in my carpet bag," Minnie said. "Could I put some of the baby's things in your trunk?"

Clair stared out the window. The busy street below reminded her of the bustle of New York City. She couldn't believe her first steps there were only a few months ago, or how far she had come in such little time.

"Clair? Are you alright, child?"

"*Pardon*? Oh, yes, just deep in thought. Do you need to put items in my travel trunk? *Bien sûre*. I do not mind."

Minnie paused the moment she opened the trunk. She fingered the quilt folded neatly on top of the other items.

"This is some quilt. Did you make it?"

"My mother did."

"May I take a look?" she asked as she gently lifted the quilt from its confinement. "Hmm," she contemplated as she held the material high and it unfurled. "So, your mother was a slave?"

"Yes. She would tell me stories of her time as a house slave in a southern plantation. Why do you ask?"

"This quilt. It looks like a map."

"A map? *Je ne comprends pas.*"

"This looks like an underground railroad map. It's different, though, because it don't got the codes that lead you to freedom up north. Usually, a map will have the white star up top to point north to freedom, but yours is at the lower right of the quilt."

"That is a piece of my baptismal dress."

"Maybe that is your white star to lead you home. You can tell it's a map of our country though. There, do you see the thirteen colorful pieces? They's in the shape of the first thirteen states. The rest of the landmass is covered in beige and purple fabric. In the middle of the quilt your mother stitched a blue thread through the country. That must be the mighty Mississippi. I saw a map once that had the river run right through the belly of the country. Then there is another blue line attached to the Mississippi, and the star is in the crook of both them rivers. I bet if we find out what river that is, you will find the people you have been looking for. I wonder if I had seen a map when we first entered the boarding house. Why don't we go down, get some supper, and look into it."

They both turned to the sleeping child in her traveling basket. Her tiny, soft fists curled under her chin, oblivious to the excitement of Clair and Minnie's present discovery.

"I would hate to disturb her sleep," Clair said. "You know best where it might be. Maybe you should look for the map and grab us some supper, Minnie. I can stay here and let the baby rest while I finish packing."

"That sounds like a good idea," Minnie said as she clasped Clair's hands. "My heart can't take in all this excitement. To think, you might find your promised land, after all!" She gave Clair's fingers a quick squeeze before releasing and rushing to the door.

After the door was closed and the rush of excitement dissipated, Clair returned to her spot near the window. Before she could even think through all that Minnie had revealed, there was a tap at the door. She turned abruptly, surprised by the unexpected noise.

"Minnie, is that you? Did you forget something?" she asked cautiously.

"Clair, I wish to speak with you," said a masculine, honey-like voice that, though muffled by the wooden barrier, sent shockwaves through her body. She stood, stunned and unable to respond.

"Please open the door," Geoffrey continued. "I would like to talk to you in person before you leave tomorrow. I need to express what is in my heart before I lose you forever."

She raced to the door, excited to hear his voice, but then paused only inches from the threshold. Her hand floated right above the doorknob, but she couldn't muster the will to turn it. She had felt their final goodbyes were enough closure, though at night she longed to hear his voice again. If she opened the door, she didn't want to endure more heartache by saying goodbye all over again. What was worse, she was more worried that the moment she saw his face, she would give up everything and forgo her travels to be with him. She was so torn her hand began to shake.

"Clair, my darling bird, you deserve to soar. To fly to a land that allows you freedom. I want to attempt to fly with you. I love you, Clair. You add color to my dull world. You give me sunshine during my dark days. I need to know how you truly feel. It's consuming me not knowing if you love me back. If you tell me you do not love me, I will leave you alone forever. But, if you tell me you feel the same, I will follow you to the ends of the Earth. I will stumble along, crossing scorched deserts or falling off the edges of the map, if that's what it takes to be with you. Please, tell me. Do you love me?"

She remained quiet and frozen. She had promised herself she would not allow anyone, especially a man, to thwart her plans. She was mad for setting herself up to fall into such an unlikely obstacle. After a few long moments, he sighed deeply.

"Whether you love me or not, I know you are strong and

determined. You worked so hard to get this far, and it is not fair to ask this of you. Just know that no matter how far you are from me, I will always love you."

Without another word, his footsteps faded down the hallway.

Her stomach tightened. She realized that the moment those footsteps were no longer heard, she'll have given up any hope of seeing him again. She not only wanted to see him, but she also wanted to keep him . . . forever. The fear of him leaving compelled her to open the door and run to him. He'd turned when her door creaked open and, without a thought, she threw herself to him and wrapped her arms around his neck. He didn't hesitate to embrace her. She buried her face against his neck, and he pressed his cheek against her hair. His fingers weaved through her loose locks that flowed down her back.

She sniffed, stifling her tears, and leaned back enough to comfortably rest her hands on his newly grown beard. She ran her fingers through bristles that blanketed his jaw, and he pressed his face against her soft touch, placing his hands over hers.

"*Mon cher amour*, my dear, dear Geoffrey," she whispered, her French accent thick with emotion. "For a long time, my only desire was to venture to the land of my mother's childhood. I did not think I would feel at home until I fulfilled what my parents wished for me, which was to find a place where I would be accepted for what and who I am. But everything changed when I met you. The moment we danced that night, I found solace in your presence. I refused to acknowledge my desire for you. I was afraid you would keep me from finding my home, but I realize now that you are my true home. I am truly myself when I am with you, and I never wish to part from you anymore. I am willing to fly alongside you."

A huge smile spread across Geoffrey's face. He leaned down to kiss her, but she gently pressed her fingertips against his lips.

"But first, m*on amour, before anything else happens, you*

need to know. I have not been completely honest with you, and I am afraid you may not forgive me for my deception."

He smiled and pressed his forehead against hers.

"You do not need to be afraid to tell me your secrets," he said.

"My father was French, that much is true, and my mother was from America. . . ."

Clair paused. This was the first time she revealed not only her secret but her mother's to someone who didn't already know. She was so accustomed to keeping it locked away that she almost couldn't force the words out. She took a steadying breath and refused to think about what would happen if Geoffrey didn't actually accept her in the end.

"My mother. . . . She was a house slave. I am not white, nor am I Black. I'm. . . . I'm. . . ."

He took hold of her chin and gently lifted her face toward his.

"You are Clair," he said gently. "You are uniquely beautiful, inside and out, and that's all you need to be. The rest does not matter to me."

He passed his thumb across her chin, searching for and caressing her lips, then pulled her close. When their lips finally met, a feeling of exuberant longing overcame them both. Their passionate kiss made them both feel like they were walking on air. With each heartbeat, they pressed closer to each other, as if needing to void any space in between themselves. She entangled her fingers through his hair, and he held onto her tightly with his strong arms. Clair felt like a bird's wings were flapping in her chest while Geoffrey felt like his entire body was on fire.

They did not care what the other guests thought as some passed them in the hallway. They ignored the sounds of the wandering or dining tenants. Geoffrey almost had a mind to carry her into her room for more privacy, but he remembered the Reverend waiting in the lobby. Reluctantly, he concluded their kiss right as they heard a baby cry.

Clair abruptly spun to return to the child, leaving

Geoffrey alone in the hallway. She came back a few moments later with the sound of Lilian whimpering in her arms. Geoffrey felt for the little hands that so readily grasped his finger. He and Clair smiled down at the precious child, and contentment overcame them as they stood side-by-side, reveling in their own tiny world filled with the people they loved the most.

Acknowledgments and Note to the Reader

I am extremely thankful for this opportunity to publish my first book; this being one of many stories that share space in my head. This would not have been possible without my faith in God and His promises to me.

I am thankful for Him giving me the gift of unique life experiences, imagination, and dreams. One of those dreams happened in 2018 that contained a girl, a blind man, a baby, an overturned carriage, and a plague.

I am thankful that He provided a supportive husband who not only proofread my first rendition but persistently cheered me on with reckless abandon. Even through the trials of my mental health struggles and learning to be a mother with ADHD, he never let me give up on my dream to become a writer. Thank you, Jeremy, for loving me unconditionally and being my safe haven.

I am thankful for my close friends and family who eagerly awaited to read every new chapter through email each week. Without their willingness to read my manuscript and their encouraging words, my procrastinating self would not have finished this book.

When I was satisfied with only my small group of readers, I reluctantly felt a calling to expand my audience. I am thankful for my librarian friend, Kim, who not only supported me through the whole writing process, but she also directed me to my favorite editor, Nicole.

I truly believe Nicole was a Godsend. She worked tirelessly not only to make the book palatable, but also to turn my childish story into a real novel. She was so patient in not only editing my book but also teaching me exceedingly more than I could have learned in a conventional way.

Furthermore, I am thankful to whoever took the time to

read this story. I am hopeful everyone enjoyed reading this book as much as I enjoyed writing it. I am thankful for your grace in noticing any potential inaccuracies in the story or flaws in my writing. My hope is to become a better writer with each novel and to have inclusive stories that offer a brief sense of home with an endless understanding of God's love for uniquely-beautiful you.

Made in United States
Orlando, FL
03 December 2024

54932759R00105